The
Golden Shadows
Old West
Museum

Number Twenty
The Texas Tradition Series
James Ward Lee, *Series Editor*

The Golden Shadows Old West Museum

A PLAY BY
Larry L. King

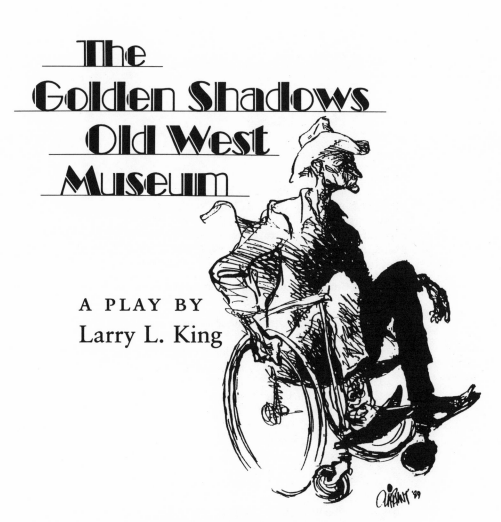

BASED ON THE SHORT STORY BY
Michael Blackman

Texas Christian University Press
FORT WORTH

Library of Congress Cataloging-in-Publication Data

King, Larry L.
    The Golden Shadows Old West Museum : a
    play / by Larry L. King.
       p. cm. — (The Texas tradition series ; no. 20)
    "Based on the short story by Michael Blackman."
    ISBN 0-87565-110-0
    I. Blackman, Michael. Golden Shadows Old
    West Museum. 1993.
  II. Title. III. Series.
  PS3561.I48G6 1993
812'.54—dc20   92-29977
               CIP

Design by Whitehead & Whitehead
Cover drawing by Pat Oliphant

The Golden Shadows Old West Museum is based on a short story by Michael Blackman. First published in *The Ohio Journal*, literary publication of Ohio State University, in 1973, "The Golden Shadows Old West Museum" was named the Best Short Story of 1973 by the Texas Institute of Letters.

Larry L. King, who wrote the stage version of *The Golden Shadows Old West Museum*, is coauthor of the hit musical comedy, *The Best Little Whorehouse in Texas*. His other plays include two off-Broadway shows, *The Kingfish* and *The Night Hank Williams Died*, and a one-act play, *Christmas: 1933*.

This book is in memory of my parents:
Clyde Clayton King and Cora Lee Clark King,
and it is for my own offspring:
Alix, Kerri, Brad, Lindsay & Blaine

Contents

Preface

MORE THAN ANY of my stage plays, *The Golden Shadows Old West Museum* seems to arouse strong, if conflicting, emotions.

It is not as simple as the play's "tugging at the heartstrings while tickling the funnybone," as one critic put it; deeper forces seem to be at work. The minority of critics who did not like the play, almost all of whom had smiled on my earlier stage offerings, seemed strident and angry beyond the call of duty. It was as if I had somehow personally offended them. While audiences have reacted favorably to *Golden Shadows* in the aggregate, some individual theater patrons told me the play depressed them, made them uncomfortable or angry or caused them to feel guilty.

I think this is because *Golden Shadows* treats a subject we all fear — the depletions of old age; most of us have witnessed time's ravages upon our parents or grandparents, a painful process at best and sometimes a cruel one.

We live in a culture where products are hawked by advertising youth, good looks, good health and vitality to the extent that growing old is by implication shameful — or at the least, bad manners. I think, too, this play depicts that impersonal treatment of old people unfortunately indigenous to too many "rest homes"; in so doing, it heightens the personal discomfort level. Those whom *Golden Shadows* made uncomfortable, or in whom it inspired guilt, usually got around to confessions of having themselves played a role in sending a beloved relative to some "senior citizens' home"; almost invariably, they were defensive and acted as if they had done something wrong.

I can identify with them. My own mother, who lived her final years in a twilight zone in which reality made only brief appearances, died of a stroke in a "rest home" less than a week after her children had reluctantly admitted her there. Although she was almost eighty-eight years old and clearly could no longer be adequately cared for in her own home, I have many times regretted that she was not permitted to die in her own bed among familiar artifacts and friendly attentions.

The first draft of this play was written only three years after my mother's 1981 death. It contains one character, Flora Harper, whose attitudes and mannerisms are loosely based on the late Cora Lee Clark King. Flora's gathering of twigs, flower cuttings and rusty relics from her yard, on the morning she was being carted off to the Golden Shadows Senior Citizens Home in mythical Leon, Texas, was directly stolen from my mother's action when, years earlier, she reluctantly moved from one old Texas farmhouse to another. The distance in miles was not great, but I now understand that my mother's uprooting cost her dearly in terms of surrendering treasured yesterdays and familiar old ground. All Golden Shadows residents in this play, except for Cowboy Bennett, have been named for my mother's relatives. And perhaps it was inevitable that as I worked, old Cowboy Bennett himself began to speak in my father's rhythms and to

utter many of Clyde Clayton King's jokes and preach-
ments; I even gave Cowboy my father's birthday.

So, obviously, this play is close to my heart — so close,
in fact, that I sometimes have to remind myself that the
basic story did not originate with me.

THE GENESIS of *The Golden Shadows Old West
Museum* traces back to 1 9 7 3 when my friend Mike
Blackman, now executive editor of *The Fort Worth Star-
Telegram*, wrote a short story by that wonderful title
while doing graduate work at Ohio State University.
Mike's story was first published in *The Ohio Journal* and
subsequently was honored by the Texas Institute of Let-
ters as the Best Short Fiction of 1 9 7 3 by a Texas writer.
In 1 9 8 6, Blackman's tale was included in *Prize Stories*,
a compilation of award-winning stories selected by the
Texas Institute of Letters, edited by Marshall Terry and
published by Still Point Press of Dallas.

Some years before that book was published — about
1979 as I recall — Roy Bode, then Washington corre-
spondent for *The Dallas Times-Herald*, mailed Mike
Blackman's short story to me with the suggestion that I
turn it into a stage play. This was hot on the heels of the
success of the musical comedy, *The Best Little Whorehouse in Texas*, which I co-authored.

I liked Mike Blackman's story, but procrastinated, as
writers will, especially one occupied by celebrating a
new hit at the expense of time spent at the typewriter. I
forgot all about the short story.

Then, in 1984, while cleaning out my desk in one of
those many gambits writers employ to avoid the key-
board on days when the words won't come, I uncovered
Mike's story and re-read it. Perhaps because I was myself
growing older, and by then had lost both my parents, the
story hit me with more impact the second time around.

Almost immediately I wrote a first draft for the stage and dispatched it to Blackman, who responded favorably. The re-writing process continued through the play's two staged readings in New York at Playwrights' Preview Productions and in Washington at New Playwrights' Theatre. *Golden Shadows* first got "on its feet" with a workshop production at Memphis State University in 1985, under the direction of Dr. Keith Kennedy, who had also helped in the development of my off-Broadway play, *The Night Hank Williams Died*. *Golden Shadows* has since received professional productions at Arkansas Repertory Theatre in Little Rock under the direction of Cliff Fannin Baker, at American Playwrights Theatre in Washington under the direction of Peter Frisch, and is scheduled for a future production at Live Oak Theatre in Austin under the direction of Don Toner.

MIKE BLACKMAN'S award-winning original short story is published within this TCU Press edition of the stage version of *The Golden Shadows Old West Museum* so that readers might see what goes into converting a narrative tale by one writer into a stage vehicle by another; the "fleshing out" of the story and the accent upon dialogue and action as opposed to the internalization of a straight narrative.

I am most grateful to my friend Mike Blackman for his planting of a good seed and hope that in his mind my subsequent spadework has not produced a disfigured tree.

LARRY L. KING
Washington, D.C.
April 1992

4

THE FIRST professional production of *The Golden Shadows Old West Museum* was at Arkansas Repertory Theatre, Little Rock, January 5-17, 1989, directed by Cliff Fannin Baker.

THE CAST

NURSE SYMMS	Julia (Cookie) Ewing
BETH GARRETT	Sara Van Horn
FLORA HARPER	Jean Ling
IDA PURVIS	Joanne Burleson
COWBOY BENNETT	Macon (Sunny) McCalman
NURSE BALDWIN	Vivian Morrison
CLAUDE	Edwin Stanfield
MISTER GASKINS	Ronald J. Aulgur

The Golden Shadows Old West Museum is a two-act, one-set play requiring a cast of five women and three men.

All action takes place in the day room of the Golden Shadows Senior Citizens Home on the outskirts of Leon, Texas.

The time is the Christmas season of 1981.

THE SETTING

Interior of the day room of the Golden Shadows Senior Citizens Home just outside the small town of Leon, Texas.

Upstage center is a wide double door permitting the passage of wheelchairs. Beyond the double door we see a portion of a hallway containing a lone cactus plant in a tall planter. Above the double door is a sign reading, "No TV past 9 P.M. Lights Out: 9:30 P.M."

Centerstage right is an old television set, its back to the audience so its screen cannot be seen. Centered in front of the television set is a worn couch. The couch faces the audience.

Downstage right is a small bookcase containing a few old books; almost none of them sport dust jackets. Four folding chairs are stacked near the bookcase; behind the folding chairs is a folded card table.

Upstage left is a nurses' station, a counter-like arrangement built in a semicircle. Behind the counter is a tall stool where a nurse sometimes presides. On the counter is a small radio, a telephone, and a name plate reading "Nurse Symms." On the wall above the nurses' station is a sign reading, "Don't Forget Your Bedtime Medication" and featuring a smiling Happy Face.

Centerstage is a tiny artificial Christmas tree, sprayed white; it rests on a small round table; the tree is rather pathetic, decorated only with a half-dozen non-electric Christmas balls. On the table are three or four gift-wrapped small packages; under the table are two larger gift-wrapped packages.

Downstage left, facing the audience, is an old over-stuffed chair. Just to the left of the chair is a magazine rack containing a few magazines and newspapers.

Action makes it obvious that actors looking over the heads of the audience are viewing a parking lot and, beyond, desert terrain visible to them through a large picture window.

The entire day room of the Golden Shadows Senior Citizens Home has a run-down look; the place obviously has seen better days.

Suggest windows showing hall beyond day room, for incidental traffic of patients, nurses, and Mr. Gaskins, to give illusion of daily life in an institution. Nurses and Mr. Gaskins can periodically look through window to check on day room activity, Claude can peek through it when hiding from Mexicans, and so on.

Act One

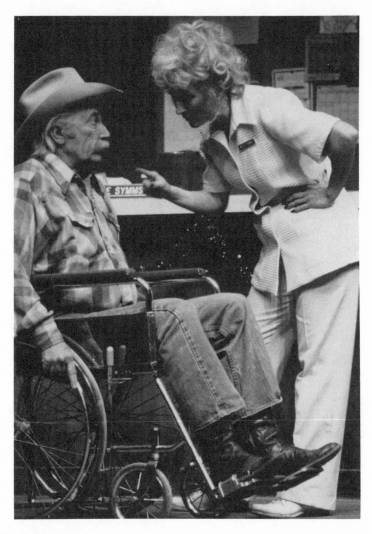

Act I, Scene 1

NURSE SYMMS (Julia Ewing): I don't wanna catch you ropin' any more of these old women, Cowboy.

COWBOY (Macon McCalman): I'll try to see you don't catch me.

Arkansas Repertory Theatre Production Little Rock 1989

Act One

Scene 1

As lights come up we see NURSE SYMMS *on the tall stool behind the nurses' station, a telephone held to her ear, issuing a shrill burst of laughter. She is a noise-maker in her mid-to-late thirties, a divorcee thrice over, with a tall beehive hairdo. An old woman,* IDA PURVIS, *chronically of dour expression, stares at the TV set from the downstage end of the couch; a single crutch rests across her legs. A second old woman,* BETH GARRETT, *birdlike and chirpy and a little addled by nature, is attempting to work the controls of the TV set without results; she slaps and shakes it lightly, though without conviction. A third old woman,* FLORA HARPER, *enters through the double door from the hall; she is a well-dressed, well-groomed lady who, despite a labored gait, transports herself with unusual dignity. She carries an ever-present big black purse. After briefly hesitating just inside the day room door, she goes to the overstuffed chair at downstage left. There, with a great hydraulic sigh, she lowers herself into the chair and stares out above the audience through the invisible*

11

picture window, *while tightly clutching her purse*
with both hands.

NURSE SYMMS

(Flirting into the telephone) Oh, you silly thing! You
know what I bet? I'll just bet your bark is a lot worse than
your bite. *(A beat; she laughs)* Now how would *you*
know how many times I've been bit, or ain't been bit,
Mister Smartie?

BETH

(Slapping TV set) Nurse Symms, I can't make this old
teevee set work. And it's time for "Our Daily Bread."

NURSE SYMMS

(Still into phone) Well, I guess that's for me to know and
for you to find out!

BETH

Nurse Symms! Somethin' is wrong with this old teevee set
again!

NURSE SYMMS

(Into telephone) Stand by, Calvin. I got one rattling her
cage. *(To Beth; irritated)* What is it *now*, Miz Garrett?

BETH

It's time for "Our Daily Bread" and I can't———

NURSE SYMMS

It is not! Supper's not for nearly three more hours.

BETH

I don't mean supper! I've hit and kicked and shook it and
everything I know to do, but I can't make it work.

NURSE SYMMS
Can't make *what* do *what*?

IDA
She can't make the goddamned television set work!

NURSE SYMMS
(Severely) Miz Purvis, you just stop your dirty talk! You
know good and well Golden Shadows is a church-affiliated institution.

IDA
Big . . . friggin' . . . deal!

NURSE SYMMS
Miz Purvis! Now if I put your nastiness in my daily
report, they might recommend you for shock treatments
or somethin'!

IDA
Do and I'll sue all your asses off!

NURSE SYMMS
(Angry) You don't even have money for a lawyer! You
don't have a thing in the whole world but what you see
here, and one little old crummy bedroom full of . . .
pictures of old dead people!

BETH
(Shocked) Oh, don't talk mean to her like that. Ida can't
help talking like she does. She's got a bad disease with a
long long name that means a person can't help cursing in
spite of theirselves.

IDA

Goddamn right!

NURSE SYMMS

Oh, sure, and if she flaps her arms she can fly like a great big bird! *(Grumbling)* Don't know why I keep puttin' up with you crazy old people. I'm half a mind to get a job at the Dairy Queen.

BETH

(In a breathless rush) We just got to get this teevee on! It's time for "Our Daily Bread," and Lisa's threatening not to come home from college for Christmas because her mama's got womb cancer and her daddy's an alcoholic infidel with a bad liver and she don't wanna tell them she's pregnant by her Arab boyfriend, who is studying to become a drama critic and a weekend terrorist.

IDA

And I don't blame her a goddam bit.

NURSE SYMMS

Miz Purvis, I'm warnin' you! One more ugly word and it all goes in my daily report! As for *you*, Miz Garrett, if I had your heart condition I wouldn't be watchin' trashy teevee shows where young white girls take up with A-rabs. Stuff like that can bring on a coronary. *(She suddenly remembers her interrupted telephone conversation)* Oh! *(Into telephone)* 'Scuse me, Calvin, I got tied up with some nutty stuff you just wouldn't believe. *(A long beat)* Hello? Calvin? *Calvin?* Hello? *(Incredulous)* That son of a bitch hung up on me!

IDA

(Laughs loudly)

NURSE SYMMS

Well, thanks to you two rattlin' on like a couple of cattle auctioneers, I've got to spend a whole quarter callin' Calvin back!

IDA

Aw, we won't tell the stingy bastards you beat 'em for a personal call.

NURSE SYMMS

(With fake sweetness) Bless your heart, you'd just *love* that, wouldn't you, Miz Purvis?

IDA

(Shrugs) No skin offa my —

BETH

(Quickly) — nose!

NURSE SYMMS

You'd run tattle to Mister Gaskins before your gown-tail hit your behind. And I'd be out of a job just in time for my three little half-orphan house apes not to have any Santa Claus this year. No, thanks! I'll just *spend* my quarter and then ask God to give y'all sick headaches. *(She comes from behind the nurses' station counter.)*

BETH

But what about this broke-down ol' teevee?

NURSE SYMMS

I'll put it in my daily report. And *if* you get lucky, and *if* the spirit moves Mister Gaskins, he'll call the repairman tomorrow.

15

BETH
Oh, fiddle! Now we'll never know what happened to Lisa on Christmas vacation.

(COWBOY BENNETT *enters speedily in his wheelchair, narrowly missing* NURSE SYMMS; *she squeals and jumps aside as he abruptly brakes. He is an old man, who always wears a cowboy hat, cowboy boots, blue jeans, a western-cut shirt and a western string tie.)*

NURSE SYMMS
Cowboy, dammit, you nearly cost me a toe!

COWBOY
Anybody that walks in the middle of the road oughta wear a stop sign.

NURSE SYMMS
(Suspicious) Are you bringin' another dern rope in here? *(She inspects his wheelchair for evidence.)*

COWBOY
Naw, sheriff, I left it in yonder by my bunk.

NURSE SYMMS
I don't wanna catch you ropin' any more of these old women, Cowboy.

COWBOY
I'll try to see you don't catch me.

(NURSE SYMMS *shakes her head and exits out the double door, turning stage left.* COWBOY *spots* FLORA *in the overstuffed chair at downstage left and slowly wheels toward her; she continues gazing blankly out the window.* IDA *takes her crutch and from her sitting position on the couch reaches out to deal the television one hard, swift blow; immediately, we hear from the TV set.)*

ACTRESS

(Voice over) All right, Muhammad. I'll call my parents tonight to break the news.

BETH

Oh, Ida, you fixed it! I wish *I* had mechanical ability.

ACTRESS

(Voice over) But, darling, I do worry how they'll react when they discover you're a registered Democrat.

COWBOY

(Over his shoulder) Will you ladies kindly turn down that infernal squall box?

(BETH quickly jumps up to turn the sound down so that it is inaudible to all except, presumably, herself and IDA; as the scene plays out, BETH and IDA react to what they are seeing and hearing on TV. COWBOY rolls his wheelchair a smidgen closer to FLORA's chair, staring intently at her. She resolutely ignores him, continuing to gaze out the window and clutch her purse with both hands.)

COWBOY

Hidy, ma'am. *(No response)* My name's Cowboy. Cowboy Bennett. *(No response)* Cowboy ain't the name my mama give me. I can't recollect my true name without checkin' my drivin' license. *(No response)* Know why everbody calls me Cowboy? *(No response. Changing his tone to indicate another person speaking)* No, Cowboy, why *does* everybody call you Cowboy?

(A beat) I bet you're thinkin' if you ignore me, I'll go on about my bidness and leave you alone. Huh? *(No response)* That's 'cause you're new here. You'll soon learn don't nobody leave you alone at Golden Shadows. The staff, heckfire, they'll wake you up in the middle of the night to give you a sleepin' pill. And they're always devilin' us to do our chores. Saves the institution a few bucks if they can git some work outta our old bones, ya see.

(A beat) You been assigned your chores yet? *(No response)* Aw, most chores ain't too bad. I don't mind checkin' the rooms twice a day to make sure somebody hadn't slipped off to Heaven unexpected.

(She glances quickly at him, then back to the window.)

What I *do* dearly despise is havin' to check three times a day to make sure everybody's flushed their commodes. *(A beat)* I can't decide if it's worse to do it before my meals, or just after.

(A beat) Know how old I am? *(No response)* No, Cowboy, how old *are* you? *(A beat)* Well, ma'am, if I live to the eighteenth day of next February, the Lord willin', I'll be eighty year old. *(No response)* Happy Birthday, Cowboy.

(A beat) You're gonna learn it's might hard to hide from folks, even if you got a private room. Which I ain't. Costs too dang much. But having a roommate's not too bad. Except when ol' Claude gits actin' crazy.

(Flora flashes him another quick look of alarm.)

I never meant to spook ya, ma'am. Claude's harmless. Now and again he gits little spells. Thinks there's a den of rattlesnakes under his bed, or that a buncha Meskins is comin' to cut his throat on account of he fought at the Alamo.

(He laughs; she attempts to edge away from him within the confines of her chair.)

Claude didn't actual *fight* at the Alamo, ya unnderstand. Even I ain't that old. *(A beat)* You oughta talk to me, ya know. I'm one of the few around here that's still got all their marbles. *(A beat)* Most of the time.

(She gives him a fearful, darting look.)

Oh, not there's anything *wrong* with me. Now and again . . . I forget a few things. Little things. Most of 'em ain't even worth rememberin'.

FLORA
(Suddenly) I do not belong here.

COWBOY
(Startled) Well . . . hello! *(No response)* I wouldn't be here myself if I hadn't got stove-up in a car wreck little over four years ago. Some dang fool had his bright lights on and blinded me, so's I turned my pickup truck over. Part of it landed on my legs. *(A beat)* Oh, I ain't a *plumb* cripple! I can dress myself and such. Just can't walk too good. *(A beat)* I never was partial to walkin' anyway. Comes from bein' horseback all my life.

FLORA
(Still staring straight ahead) By no stretch of the imagination do I belong here. There has been a . . . mistake, that's all. A mistake.

COWBOY

Yes, ma'am.

FLORA

Sooner or later someone of responsibility will discover that mistake. And then I'll be free as . . . *(She waves toward the invisible picture window.)* . . . as those birds flying around out there.

COWBOY

(Looking out the window) I'm afraid them's buzzards, ma'am.

FLORA

(Hand to breast) Oh! *(Weakly)* I simply . . . do not belong here.

COWBOY

(Not unkindly) Bet your own kids put you in this place.

(She looks at him sharply, then quickly redirects her gaze out the window.)

Most likely your husband died. And purty soon your kids started sayin' you maybe had gone downhill a little. Said you forgot things . . . and was by yourself too much . . . and your house was too big for you to keep up . . . and they was afraid you might fall and break a hip. Huh? *(No response)* So after a while they helt a little pow-wow and decided you'd be better off in a place like this. With people your own age for company . . . people paid to look after you . . . and a doctor on the staff in case you got sick sudden. *(A beat)* And when your kids come to tell you about it, they tried to make it sound like you was goin' on a pleasure cruise and would have more fun than at the goddern circus.

(She turns to look really hard at COWBOY *for the first time, astonished that he knows so much of her story.)*

Don't look so flabbergasted, ma'am. You sure don't hold no patent on *that* story.

(She quickly looks away; he attempts to lighten the mood.)

Whatcha got in that purse? Fort Knox? *(No response)* Rumor's already goin' around you got your whole life savin's in that purse. On account of the way you swing on to it. *(No response)* You got a name?
(No response) How I come to be called Cowboy — and I'm sure glad you asked — is because I *was* one. And not one of them sissy singin' movie cowboys, neither. Why, thunder, that movie and teevee bunch wouldn't know how to turn a bull into a steer! *(He laughs.)* Yessum, for years I was a workin' cowboy. Lived in a old line shack up yonder about two hours by horseback above Amarillo. On the Flying W spread. Winter times, I might not lay eyes on nobody but cattle and critters for weeks at a time. A man does that, after a while, he'll get so he talks to hisself. *(A beat; wryly)* Kinda like I'm doin' now.

(She gives him another quick look.)

Ain't nothin' wrong in talkin' to yourself. At least you git the satisfaction of listenin' to somebody with good sense. *(A beat)* Course when me and Erleane got married I had to give up that line shack and move in a regular house there at the main ranch. That's when I commenced specializin' in green stock, which, if ya don't know, is horses that hadn't never been saddle broke. People come from all over for me to break their green stock. I didn't give a hoot *what* a horse done: he could sunfish, fenceline, or take the high dive. Wadn't a horse on this earth too rank for Cowboy Bennett in them days.

(A beat) Feller that owned the Flying W spread was gettin' six prices for me to break them broncs, while he set in a rockin' chair. All I got was bruises and a cowhand's wages. Forty dollar a month and found, back then. So I quit and commenced rodeoin'. *(A beat)* You heard of that big rodeo over at Stamford, hadn't you? That Cowboy Reunion Rodeo? *(No response)* Sure you have. Everybody in Texas knows about that Cowboy Reunion Rodeo. And the one at the Fat Stock Show down in Fort Worth. They still recollect Cowboy Bennett in them places, sure do. *(A beat)* The old ones do anyhow. *(A beat)* The ones that ain't dead.

BETH
(Reacting to TV story) Oh, Ida, this is just so sad!

COWBOY
(Misunderstanding; irritated) Ain't nothin' sad about it! Everbody gets old and everbody dies. It's just . . . nature's way.

(BETH and IDA look startled, and then exchange shrugs and continue watching TV.)

There was a ol' outlaw horse went by the name of 'Widder Maker.' That horse hadn't *never* been rode. Mean as a hard-dollar banker, that horse was. He'd try to bite your leg off in the chute! And if he put you on the ground, why he'd try to stomp you to packed dirt. *(He laughs)* One time back in 19-and-27 I drawed ol' Widder Maker there at that Cowboy Reunion Rodeo. Folks made up a *terrible* pota money, bettin' this way and that. I had a big followin' in them days!

(A beat) Course, now, ol' Widder Maker did too. I expect he was nearly as famous as Jack Dempsey. Er-leane, she begged me not to even *try* ridin' that killer horse. Said 'Never was a rider that couldn't be throwed.' And I come right back with, 'Never was a horse that couldn't be rode.' *(Enthused)* Me and ol' Widder Maker, we exploded outta that chute like a five-dollar fire-cracker! That ol' horse pulled ever trick under the *sun* tryin' to git shed of me. And by ginnies, I *rode* 'im.

(He rares back in his wheelchair, sits as erectly as possible, and puffs with pride.) Two-and-a-half *minutes*! Course, now, they quit keepin' official time long before that, 'cause most horses will either buck you off sooner or quit buckin'. But that hammerhead kept on buckin' and I rode him to a standstill till he *did* quit. Broke *all* the stubborn outa that horse! *(A beat)* In a way, I hated that. There's something *wrong* about taking the fight outta a high-spirited critter. Whether its got four legs or two.

IDA
(Reacting to TV) Oh, what a crock of crap! Can't she tell when he's lying to her?

COWBOY
(Again misunderstanding; angry) No such dang thing! I take a paralyzed oath or lightnin' can strike me dead!

(FLORA *flinches at this outburst;* COWBOY *calms himself.)*

23

You ought to of heard them people cheerin'. Why folks whooped and hollered like I was some kind of war hero! I reckon that was just about the high-water mark of my life.

BETH

(Reacting to TV) Oh, I don't think I can *stand* any more of this sad stuff!

COWBOY

(Sharply) Then leave the dang room ! I ain't even talkin' to you!

IDA

And she ain't talking to *you*, you silly old fart!

COWBOY

(Befuddled) Oh . . . . *(To Flora)* Anyhow, for ridin' old Widder Maker I got a special saddle give to me by the rodeo association. I'd have it here in my room, along with my spurs and brandin' irons and bridles and all the cowboy gear I got in there now ... except I lost it. *(A beat)* Lost it in a poker game to my sorry brother-in-law, back when I was a bad hand to drink. Just goes to show you that whiskey and cards don't mix.

FLORA

I wouldn't know about such things.

COWBOY

Well, hello again!

FLORA

(Hesitating) Hello.

COWBOY

(Enthused) That saddle, see, it had a *world* of silver platin' on it. Why, it shined like a new dime! And carved on it in big letters was "All Around Champion Cowboy." *(He drags a hand through the air in a long line, as if describing a theater marquee.)* All Around Champion Cowboy. And right underneath that was my name. *(A beat)* Ya know, if I still had that saddle I'd put it with my cowboy gear and open me a museum right here in this place. Charge people two bits a head to come see it and hear me tell what it was like bein' a *real* cowboy. All folks knows about now is them silly movie and teevee cowboys. Why, most of 'em couldn't ride a dang stickhorse!

(A beat) Know what I'd call it? Huh? *(Flora shakes her head.)* The Golden Shadows Old West Museum. Whatta ya think of that? *(No response)* Might even post me some signs up yonder on Highway 80, by the Big Springs cutoff, directin' the public down here to it.

FLORA

Mister Bennett, there's something you should know about me.

COWBOY

Well . . . sure. What is it?

FLORA

I hold no brief for rodeos . . . or rodeo people.

COWBOY

(Staring at her) That mean . . . you don't like them?

FLORA

No offense, sir, but that would be putting it mildly.

COWBOY

(Spluttering) Why that's . . . that's . . . I never heard of such! Rodeo's just as American as apple pie. Maybe more so here in Texas!

FLORA

I have my reasons.

COWBOY

Well, I can't imagine what they'd be! You a foreigner or somethin'?

FLORA

I lost my first husband . . . to a blonde . . . "hussy" who was a rodeo trick rider.

COWBOY

A barrel rider? (He laughs.) Why, shoot, ma'am, I run with half a dozen of them barrel-ridin' gals myself!

(She turns her head away, offended; he tries to recover.)

Course, now, I always come *back* just as soon as . . . . *(He trails off, embarrassed.)* I take it your husband . . . didn't.

FLORA

(Severely) Indeed he did not!

COWBOY

Well . . . good riddance, most likely! *(She gives him a questioning look.)* You did say he was your *first* husband? *(She nods.)* So you found yourself another feller! So what'd you lose? *(No response)* How many husbands you had altogether?

FLORA

(Haughtily) Only two, thank you!

COWBOY

No need to git your stinger out, ma'am, I just . . . .

FLORA

And I'm *not* lookin' for another.

COWBOY

Me neither.

(She half smiles, then turns away so he won't see it — but he already has.)

The one good thing about your fire goin' out is that you won't git burnt no more.

(She gasps and turns her head away; he again tries to make up.)

Uh, lissen, ma'am. I don't mean no harm. I hadn't been around a real lady in so long, I . . . sometimes I forget my manners. *(No response)* Say now, I'm on the chore committee! I'll be glad to put in a word to see you git some nice, easy chore. *(No response)* But naturally I can't do that unless . . . .

(He leaves it dangling; she gives him a look.)

FLORA

Unless . . . ?

27

COWBOY
Unless I know your name.

(She hides a small smile.)

FLORA
Mrs. Harper . . . Mrs. Ben D. Harper

COWBOY
How long has . . . Ben Harper been dead?

FLORA
Almost three years. *(She tears up.)*

COWBOY
Then don't you think maybe it's time to start usin' your own name? *(No response)* Lemme guess what it is. *(A beat)* Sara? Naw. That's a little too old-fashioned. Maggie? Naw, naw. Somethin' a little more *re*-fined. *(A beat)* You look kinda like a *Christine* to me. Bet folks call you "Crissie." *(He produces a folded red bandana from his pocket and extends it; she takes it and wipes her eyes.)* Am I right?

(She shakes her head in the negative.)

Wanta gimme a hint?

(She offers a ghost of a smile.)

FLORA
It's . . . Flora.

COWBOY
Flora. Well, now . . . that'll do.

FLORA

I've never liked it. I wanted to be named . . . Laura or Katherine. I suppose that's rather silly.

COWBOY

Aw, I wouldn't say that! *(Looks around, furtively)* Just between me and you, if I wadn't called "Cowboy," I'd wanta be called "Bart."

(She smiles her first full smile.)

Tell ya what, Flora. I'll go over that chore list, and we'll pick out somethin' nice and easy. Then I'll speak to the chore committee.

FLORA

(Returning his bandana) That's very kind and considerate. But it won't be necessary.

COWBOY

The devil it won't! You wouldn't wanta git stuck helpin' to haul out the garbage, or . . . or helpin' poke pills down some old codger that might bite your fingers!

FLORA

You don't understand. *(She stares out the window, visibly tightening her grip on her purse.)* I do not . . . belong . . . here.

(Cowboy tentatively reaches out as if to commiserate but thinks better of it and slowly withdraws his hand, as lights go down to blackout.)

Scene 2

(From the dark we hear the sound of a country-western tune coming to a close; as the lights come up we see NURSE SYMMS *on the stool behind the nurses' station counter, vigorously filing her fingernails and just as vigorously chewing gum, as she listens to the radio.)*

RADIO ANNOUNCER

(Voice over) Only four more days till Christmas, neighbors, and wouldn't it be a doggone shame if your family woke up to find that ol' Santa has left 'em driving the same old klunker? Broncho Reconditioned Vehicles, at 1608 West Yucca, wants to help you *avoid* that. Broncho's prices have been slashed so doggone low the owner's wife may have to take a part-time job. But she's willing to do that to help put you and yours behind the wheel of a sparkling fixed-up, painted-up reconditioned vehicle that'll look so doggone good your neighbors will think it came straight from De-troit to you. All makes, all models, all colors, and all *right*! The folks at Broncho are asking such little money down you're gonna think they're joking — and, your first easy monthly installment won't

be due until February 1st. Come in today to take advantage of the amazing Santa Claus specials at Broncho Reconditioned Vehicles, 2608 West Yucca, smack-dab in the heart of downtown Sweetwater. *(A beat)* Now here's the ol' Texas Troubadour, Ernest Tubb, to tell us what it's like "Walkin' the Floor Over You."

(We hear that song begin as NURSE BALDWIN, *a young woman in her twenties, pushes a wheelchair into the day room from the hall; the wheelchair contains a large package wrapped in brown shipping paper and plastered with Christmas seals.)*

NURSE SYMMS

That for me?

NURSE BALDWIN

Don't you wish! It's for Cowboy.

NURSE SYMMS

Cowboy? I never knew him to get nothin' but ties he won't wear. *(She reaches over and turns off the radio.)* Wonder what in the world that *is?*

NURSE BALDWIN

Well, it weighs enough to be a solid lead bedpan. *(Grunting, she shoves the package under the table holding the small Christmas tree.)*

NURSE SYMMS

I'd give a Yankee dime to know what's in that big ol' thing!

NURSE BALDWIN

(Crossing) This letter came with it.

NURSE SYMMS

You think the letter tells?

NURSE BALDWIN

It's plastered with so many Christmas seals it might take a crowbar to open it.

NURSE SYMMS

(Looking at the package) I got a better idea.

NURSE BALDWIN

(Following her gaze) Oh, No! There's a *law* against opening other people's mail.

NURSE SYMMS

You mean to tell me you ain't the least bit curious?

NURSE BALDWIN

No. Not really.

(NURSE SYMMS *gives her a wide, disbelieving grin.*)

Well . . . maybe a smidgen.

NURSE SYMMS

Look at it this way: there could be somethin' in that big package that might over-excite Cowboy. You *know* he won't hardly take his Lithium, which is why he's so cranked-up all the time. Now as his *nurses*, don't you think we've got a medical duty to make sure there ain't somethin' in that package that might be bad for our patient?

NURSE BALDWIN

Selma, you *know* we're not medical nurses. We're just glorified babysitters.

NURSE SYMMS

Don't Mister Gaskins and Doctor Gilbert call Cowboy and the others our "patients"?

NURSE BALDWIN

Well, yeah —

NURSE SYMMS

Don't they call us "Nurse" Symms and "Nurse" Baldwin?

NURSE BALDWIN

Yeah, but —

NURSE SYMMS

Didn't we have to take a two-week first-aid course before we could work here?

NURSE BALDWIN

Yes, but —

NURSE SYMMS

So, screw it. We're *nurses*! Now run over there by the door and stand lookout.

NURSE BALDWIN

Oh my God, that makes it sound like we're robbing a bank!

(NURSE SYMMS *rummages under the counter, producing a letter opener and a roll of tape;* NURSE BALDWIN *pushes the wheelchair to the double door to assume her lookout's duties.*)

Cowboy's likely to scream bloody murder if he finds out.

NURSE SYMMS

(Crossing to package) He won't find out! I'll slit one end
of the package open real careful, then tape it back good
after we've had a peep.

NURSE BALDWIN

What if you rip it?

NURSE SYMMS

Then we'll blame the damned post office!

(NURSE BALDWIN's *head twists left to right, in con-
stant motion, as she nervously looks up and down
the hall;* NURSE SYMMS *conducts her surgical oper-
ation with the letter opener.)*

NURSE BALDWIN

If I see somebody coming, do I whistle, or what?

NURSE SYMMS

Now why would you *whistle?* Just speak to whoever it
is real normal. You got plenty of time — that hall is half
as long as a football field.

NURSE BALDWIN

I was thinking how *short* it looks. *(A beat; nervously)* I
saw Cowboy and that new old woman, Flora, in the
cafeteria when I passed. Sure hope they don't decide to
come in here.

NURSE SYMMS

Do you believe how he's trailed that stuck-up old biddy
around all week? I told Cowboy he's makin' a fool out
of hisself, but he got mad and threatened to rope me. The
old boy's got a sure 'nuff case of sweet-ass. *(A beat)* Do
you think people that old . . . still do it?

NURSE BALDWIN
(Nervously) Do what?

NURSE SYMMS
Now whatta you *think* I mean?

NURSE BALDWIN
I'm too nervous to think.

NURSE SYMMS
There useta be a old man here, I caught him in bed one time with old Miz Lasater. The old fool had the trap door of his long handles open, and the two of 'em was laying there in her bed giggling like a couple of kids playin' doctor.

NURSE BALDWIN
(Intrigued) Really? What happened?

NURSE SYMMS
He died.

NURSE BALDWIN
From *that*?

NURSE SYMMS
No, you ninny, from being ninety-seven! *(A beat)* I don't see how old people can even stand to kiss each other, much less actually *do* it. I feel the same way about ugly things like turtles and snakes tryin' to get it on.

NURSE BALDWIN
Don't waste so much time talking, Selma!

NURSE SYMMS
Well, don't *you* keep turnin' your head like you're watchin' a tennis match! I never saw anybody so suspi-

cious-lookin' in my life! *(She now has gained entry to one end of the package and peers in.)* What in the name of sweet precious Jesus?

NURSE BALDWIN

(Alarmed) What?

NURSE SYMMS

It's a damned rockin' horse! Why would anybody send an old man a kiddie's damned *rockin'* horse?

NURSE BALDWIN

Could it be some kind of a joke? I mean, since people call him "Cowboy" —

NURSE SYMMS

It's a joke all right. And the joke's on us. They put cowboy's gift in an old used box. And it's got more tape on it than one of them damned Egyptian mummies like I seen in the movies.

NURSE BALDWIN

Hurry up and tape it back! This kinda stuff makes me nervous.

NURSE SYMMS

(Dryly) No shit?

NURSE BALDWIN

Well, I for one was not brought up to be a meddling sneak.

NURSE SYMMS

Yeah. Your mama would be real proud of how hard you worked at talkin' me outta this.

(NURSE BALDWIN *suddenly stiffens as she looks down the hall to stage right, then begins to wave frantically as if trying to flag down a bus.*)

NURSE BALDWIN

(*Calling loudly*) Hi, Cowboy, Hi, Miz-uh-Miz-uh Flora! How y'all today? Sure good to see you! I got to run now! Time to make my rounds! Bye bye!

NURSE SYMMS

Jesus! Judas was a *lap dog* compared to you!

(*She makes frantic repairs, then hurries to the nurses' station to hide the tape and letter opener.* COWBOY *wheels in;* FLORA HARPER, *clutching her purse, walks beside him.*)

COWBOY

That nurse havin' a runnin' fit?

NURSE SYMMS

(*Too sweetly*) Oh, hi, Cowboy! And how you today, Miz Harper?

COWBOY

I had a huntin' dog that throwed runnin' fits. Name of Old Blue. That old dog —

NURSE SYMMS

Cowboy, a letter just come for you.

COWBOY

Huh? A letter? For me?

NURSE SYMMS

(*Crossing with letter*) Yep. You got a package, too.

COWBOY
Then where's the package at?

NURSE SYMMS
Under the tree. That big brown one.

COWBOY
(Looking) Well, I'll be switched! Reckon what that is?

NURSE SYMMS
I would have no way of knowing. *(A beat)* Want me to
read your letter to you?

COWBOY
Why? I can read.

NURSE SYMMS
Well, considerin' your cataracts —

COWBOY
Never mind my cataracts. My cataracts is my own dang
bidness.

NURSE SYMMS
Well, may I *drop dead* for tryin' to do you a good deed!

(She flounces back to her station; COWBOY *wheels
down near the overstuffed chair where* FLORA *is
seating herself.)*

COWBOY
Flora, would you just *look* at that big package? I usually
don't git nothin' but socks and ties and such. *(He starts
to open his letter, then has a sudden thought.)* Why,
thunderation, I bet I know what's in that package!

NURSE SYMMS

You do?

COWBOY

(To FLORA; *enthused)* Used to be a old feller here — he's dead now — had him a three-speed electric wheelchair. Why, that chair could zip around like a dang race car! I sure did admire that three-speed chair and wanted one like it. I had a notion, ya see, to hook up other people's wheelchairs behind me. Kinda like a long train? And then I'd go toot-tootin' through this place and drive the staff plumb nuts. *(He laughs)*

FLORA

(Amused) Oh, Mister Bennett!

COWBOY

Well, now, when that old man died, I told my daughter she oughta buy that chair for me from his kids. She wouldn't do it, but I bet she's changed her mind and bought me one of them three-speed chairs! *(He enthusiastically rips open his letter)*

FLORA

Perhaps you shouldn't count on it.

COWBOY

Naw, naw, that package is just about the right size to hold a three-speed wheelchair all folded up! *(He unfolds his letter and then, attempting to get the print into focus, moves it at varying distances back and forth in front of his face.)*

NURSE SYMMS

Why, Cowboy, I didn't know you could play the trombone!

(COWBOY glares back over his shoulder as she laughs; he then extends the letter to FLORA.)

COWBOY

I'd be much obliged if you'd . . . .

FLORA

(Taking the letter) Of course. *(A beat)* It's signed "Eloise."

COWBOY

That's my daughter all right. She's sent me that three-speed electric wheelchair!

FLORA

"Dear Papa: Don't you dare open your package until Christmas Day, and don't you give the Golden Shadows authorities a difficult time about waiting. I think you'll find the wait well worth it, as this is something you have wanted for a long time . . . . "

COWBOY

See there! That's it! It's my three-speed chair!

FLORA

(Again reading) "Bruce has a state bar association meeting in San Antonio right after the holidays, and he must prepare a speech for it, so . . . *(She pauses for a couple of beats.)* . . . so it looks as if we won't be able to see you for the holidays, as much as we regret it." *(She glances at COWBOY, then resumes reading.)* "Be sure to eat all your meals, and do exactly as the doctors and nurses say. They are professionals, and they are there to help you, so heed their advice and suggestions. Remember not to eat jalapeno peppers, chili, and other hot, spicy foods as they

41

give people your age heartburn. I'll try to call you some-
time during the holidays, if not Christmas Day itself, and
hope to find you well. Love from all of us, Eloise." *(A
beat)* Well, that's . . . a very . . . nice letter.

COWBOY

Last year he was gettin' ready for some big courtroom
trial. *(A beat)* Year before that . . . I can't recollect now . . .
what it was.

FLORA

I suppose young career people stay very busy in this day
and age.

COWBOY

Yeah. Seems so.

*(She extends the letter; he absently returns it to the
envelope.)*

FLORA

One of my sons, and his wife, may be able to get here
Christmas afternoon. There's nothing definite, but —
well, *if* they should, perhaps you would consent to join
us for dinner. At a cafe.

COWBOY

That's mighty nice. But I . . . just never cottoned to cafe
cookin'. Much obliged anyway. *(Trying to rally)* I got
worlds to do around here that day, ya see. Bein' on the
Christmas committee and . . . all.

FLORA

Well, judging by its size, that certainly is an impressive
gift your daughter sent.

42

COWBOY

Yeah.

FLORA

I don't believe I've ever seen a three-speed electric wheelchair, Mister Bennett. *(No response)* You must be ter-
ribly excited at the prospect of getting one.

COWBOY

Naw. Anybody that'd warn you against eatin' chili and
hot peppers wouldn't send you a chair such as that.

FLORA

Well, it's fun to speculate. *(No response)* Mister Bennett,
would you care to play a game of checkers? Or dominoes,
perhaps? They tell me you're quite accomplished at dominoes.

COWBOY

Tell the truth, I think I drunk a little too much of that rich
cocoa. Made me kinda drowsy. I might better . . . go take
my nap. *(He starts wheeling slowly away.)*

NURSE SYMMS

Hold it, Cowboy! You hadn't took your Lithium in three
or four days. *(She crosses to him, carrying a glass of
water, and hands* COWBOY *a pill; he hesitates, looking at
it.)* Don't make me poke it down you.

*(He pops the pill in his mouth, takes the water, and
drinks it down.)*

See, that didn't harelip you, now, did it? Why can't you
be a good boy like that all the time?

(COWBOY wordlessly wheels toward the double doors and exits; NURSE SYMMS looks after him for a couple of beats.)

What's with him? One minute he's John Wayne and the next minute he's a pussycat. I guess I won't ever understand you old folks until I'm . . . as old as you are.

FLORA

(Rising) On that you may count, my dear. On that you most *assuredly* may count.

(She crosses toward the exit; NURSE SYMMS gapes after her and shrugs.)

NURSE SYMMS

Fruitcakes. Everybody around this place is a walkin' damn fruitcake!

(Lights go down to blackout)

Scene 3

(From the dark we hear faint strains of some tra-
ditional Christmas carols with a Muzak sound. As
lights come up we see COWBOY *asleep in his wheel-*
chair near the picture window downstage; in the
early part of the scene he will snore occasionally,
moan or mutter without anyone paying attention.
NURSE SYMMS *is listlessly placing strands of silvery*
tinsel on the small Christmas tree. NURSE BALDWIN
enters carrying a tray of medications; she crosses to
place it on the nurses' station counter.)

NURSE BALDWIN

Mister Gaskins says be sure everybody takes their bedtime medication tonight. He don't want the patients
climbing the walls at the Christmas party tomorrow.

NURSE SYMMS

Last year, while Mister Gaskins was playing Santa Claus,
some old woman got so keyed up she peed on his britches
leg.

*(*NURSE BALDWIN *laughs.)*

It was abso-goddamn-lutely the highlight of my Golden
Shadows career.

(NURSE BALDWIN *crosses to help decorate the tree.*)

NURSE BALDWIN
Have you been a good girl this year, Nurse?

NURSE SYMMS
Hunny, I been such a good girl I been thinkin' about shootin' myself.

NURSE BALDWIN
(Grinning) Then what's Santa gonna bring you?

NURSE SYMMS
If I had my druthers, he'd bring me double child-support payments and a tall handsome stranger with marriage on his mind.

NURSE BALDWIN
Where would that leave Calvin?

NURSE SYMMS
Where he belongs. At home with his wife.

(NURSE BALDWIN *laughs.*)

Remember when you was a little kid, how excited you got about Christmas?

NURSE BALDWIN
Oh, yeah. Counting the days, not being able to sleep the night ol' Santa was coming.

NURSE SYMMS
That was *then.* Nowadays at Christmas time I get so depressed I wish I had a dog, just so I could kick it.

NURSE BALDWIN

(Amused) Oh, Selma, don't be such an old bah-hum-
bugger.

NURSE SYMMS

Easy enough for *you* to say. You got half a dozen young
men pantin' after you. *I* got a houseful of rug rats to gripe
and moan when Santa don't bring 'em gold watches and
sports cars. *(A beat)* I don't know how much longer I can
scrape by on this Mickey Mouse salary. I asked Mister
Gaskins for a raise last month, but he preached a sermon
about the obligation of the church to feed starvin' kids
in Africa. I said, "Mister Gaskins, what's the church got
against feedin' starvin' kids in Leon, Texas?"

NURSE BALDWIN

You didn't!

NURSE SYMMS

Hell I didn't!

NURSE BALDWIN

What did he say?

NURSE SYMMS

It didn't seem to be in English. *(She steps back to regard
the Christmas tree critically.)* Well, I'd hoped these icicles
might perk up this sorry old tree, but they're just makin'
it look like a dimestore weepin' willow.

NURSE BALDWIN

It sure would look better with a string of electric lights.

NURSE SYMMS

No chance. Mister Gaskins is afraid this dump might burn down. And I'm afraid it *won't*. *(Sighs)* I don't know why we bother. Half the patients won't know if it's Christmas or the Fourth of July, and the other half always get the blues from rememberin' better Christmases.

NURSE BALDWIN

We bother, Selma, because we're about all these old people have.

NURSE SYMMS

Then they're in a helluva fix, ain't they?

NURSE BALDWIN

Sometimes I think you're the sourest person I ever met! Don't you feel *sorry* for the old people here? They're at the end of their roads, Selma. And for most of them it's a bumpy ride.

NURSE SYMMS

Aw, I know. But they give me the blues. I can't *help* that. Especially at Christmas. We're supposed to run around grinnin' and full of fake happiness, like this ain't the saddest place short of a funeral home.

NURSE BALDWIN

But some of these old people are getting as excited about the party as little kids!

NURSE SYMMS

This is your first year here, hunny. Come talk to me next Christmas.

MISTER GASKINS

(Voice over) Attention, all nursing personnel. Those nurses not currently engaged in essential activities will report immediately to the administrator's office for the daily staff briefing.

NURSE BALDWIN

Oh, foot! That's the biggest waste of time! All he does is tell corny jokes.

NURSE SYMMS

And talk about how we've got to cut costs to the bone so we can feed starving pickaninnies.

(NURSE BALDWIN *starts to the hall, turns and looks back at* NURSE SYMMS, *who is still desultorily decorating the tree.*)

NURSE BALDWIN

That's an essential activity?

NURSE SYMMS

Whos gonna know? I could be givin' some patient mouth-to-mouth.

NURSE BALDWIN

Oh, come along! He might give out Christmas bonuses.

NURSE SYMMS

Ha! You dreamer!

NURSE BALDWIN

Well, *if* we get Christmas bonuses, the rumor is that they'll be handed out at today's staff meeting.

(NURSE SYMMS *hesitates, looks at the remaining ici-cles in her hand, shrugs, and throws the entire hand-ful willy-nilly at the tree. They exit down the hall, turning stage left. For a few beats we hear nothing but* COWBOY *snoring. Then* CLAUDE *rushes in from the hall towards stage right. He is an old man in pajamas and houseshoes and has a blanket draped over his shoulders.*)

CLAUDE

Cowboy! Wake up, Cowboy! They're here. *(He rushes down to shake* COWBOY *awake.)* They're comin' after me, Cowboy, I saw them in the parking lot.

COWBOY

(Waking; befuddled) What horse did I draw, Lefty? *(Focusing on* CLAUDE*)* God dang it, *you* ain't Lefty!

CLAUDE

Well, a-course I'm not!

COWBOY

Do you know what horse I drawed?

CLAUDE

Cowboy, it's *me*! Claude!

COWBOY

Oh. Claude. *(He rubs his eyes.)* I reckon I had a dream.

CLAUDE

You gotta help me, Cowboy! There's a whole truckload of Mexicans after me! I saw 'em gettin' outta that truck on the parking lot! *(He rushes to stare out the window.)*

COWBOY

(Weary) Claude, there ain't no Meskins.

CLAUDE

Of course there's Mexicans! Texas is full of Mexicans!

(BETH *and* IDA *enter from the hall,* IDA *walking with one crutch.)*

COWBOY

But there ain't no Meskins *here*! There ain't a dozen Meskins in this whole dang county.

CLAUDE

Cowboy, I *saw* 'em! They even parked in my parking space.

COWBOY

Claude, you ain't *got* a parkin' space. You ain't got a *car* no more.

(BETH *comes downstage and looks out the picture window.)*

CLAUDE

If you'd helped me build a moat around this place, like I wanted to, it'd protect us from Mexicans and rattle-snakes both.

COWBOY

(Conciliatory) Maybe we'll build it next week, Claude.

BETH

Mister Yeager, the only truck out yonder is Preacher Jordan's pick-up truck.

CLAUDE

(Rushing to the window) How do you know it's his?

BETH

Because one bumper sticker says, "Love thy Neighbor" and the other one says, "Kill a Commie for Christ."

CLAUDE

Them Mexicans will kill *me* if they catch me! They've had it in for me ever since I fought at the Alamo.

COWBOY

Dang it, Claude, you never fought at the Alamo!

CLAUDE

(Eagerly) Will you tell them Mexicans that?

IDA

If you'd fought at the Alamo, you wouldn't be alive unless *you* was a Mexican, you dumbass!

CLAUDE

I was the only one that escaped, and they know it!

COWBOY

Go hide in your room, Claude. I'll get rid of the Meskins for you.

CLAUDE

You're a true pal, Cowboy. *(He shakes* COWBOY*'s hand feverishly.)* I'll buy you a drink soon as this seige is over. *(He rushes out, pulling his blanket over his head, and exits down the hall towards stage right.)*

IDA

Crazy old coot. He comes near me, I'll brain him with my damn crutch.

COWBOY

Claude's just havin' one of his spells.

BETH

Yes, Ida, and on his good days, Mister Yeager is a very smart man. Why I bet he's as smart as . . . the President of the United States.

IDA

Shit, who ain't?

BETH

Oh, Cowboy, I nearly forgot! Mister Gaskins said to tell you the Christmas committee's meeting in the cafeteria to make last-minute plans.

COWBOY

I quit that fool committee.

BETH

Quit? Why . . . you're the chairman!

IDA

Know *why* the old fool quit? 'Cause they wouldn't put his new sweetheart on that damn commitee, and it got his nose out of joint.

COWBOY

No such thing! I just . . . ain't got time to mess with that dang committee.

IDA

(Harsh laugh) Ya don't have a friggin' thing *but* time. And ya don't know how long that's gonna last.

COWBOY

Well, I ain't got time to put up with some old . . . *cow* mooin' and bellerin'! *(He wheels rapidly and angrily toward the door.)*

IDA

(Calling after him) Where ya going? To polish that imaginary *saddle* you're always blowin' about?

COWBOY

(Stopping and wheeling to face her) I won that saddle fair and square for ridin' Old Widder Maker in 19-and-29.

IDA

One day you say 19-and-29, one day you say 19-and-27, one day you say somethin else again. You know what *I* say? *I* say it's all bullshit.

COWBOY

(Angry) Somedays I can't rightly recollect *when* it happened, but it *did* happen! *(A beat; calmer)* I know for dang sure . . . it happened. I can see it in my mind like it was . . . yesterday.

BETH

I believe you, Cowboy.

IDA

Oh, and do you believe in the tooth fairy?

(COWBOY's *had enough; he wheels away rapidly and exits.*)

BETH

(*Angry and feisty*) Ida, I believe you're the meanest old woman in the world! Why do you *work* at being mean? What do you get out of it?

(IDA *looks away from her.*)

How come you don't like *anybody*, Ida?

IDA

'Cause nobody likes *me!*

(*She bursts into tears.* BETH *is stunned. She approaches* IDA *and uncertainly touches her on the shoulder.*)

BETH

Oh, Ida, that's not true. *I* like you. A lot of people would like you, if you would only let them.

IDA

(*Snuffling*) No, they wouldn't.

BETH

Oh, now, honey —

IDA

I don't think my damned husband even liked me. I lived with Troy Purvis for forty-four years and made him as good a wife as I knew how. Washed his clothes, cooked his meals, raised five of his children. Dragged from one old oil-field camp to another with him, living in shacks and tents and . . . places not fit for a damn dog. I didn't fuss or whine anymore'n the average. Just bit my tongue and hoped for better someday . . . long past when I knew better was never likely to come. And do you think that man ever once said, "Ida, I *like* you" or "Ida, I *appreciate* you"? In a pig's ass he did! Just . . . gobbled his meals without knowing what he was eating — it coulda been the oilcloth, it coulda been a old *shoe*, as long as it had ketchup on it — and swilled his beer and tumbled into bed without a word. Dammit, he could've said *something*.

BETH

(Gently) Ida, did you ever tell your husband . . . that you liked him? Or *loved* him?

IDA

(After a beat) No. Not in so many words.

BETH

(Softly) Why not?

IDA

Why should I have? *(She looks away; softer)* I've always . . . had trouble . . . saying candy-assed things to people.

BETH

Maybe your husband did too, Ida. He *did* stay with you for forty-four years. *(No response)* A lot of us probably take too much for granted as we hurry through our lives. There's always a living to make, always bills to pay, always something to keep us on the run. We don't know how short the race is . . . until it's over. *(A beat)* Sometimes I wish I had hugged my babies more when they were little. Maybe if I had . . . they'd hug me a little more now.

IDA

You could have hugged your damn kids till it bruised 'em, and things wouldn't be different now. People don't give back what they get. Haven't you learned *that* much?

BETH

I don't claim to be a smart woman, but I do know the things we'd like to do over . . . are the things we can't do over. If I read the Bible right, I think we have to learn to forgive each other . . . even forgive ourselves . . . for slights and mistakes along the way.

IDA

One thing Troy Purvis did to me . . . I can *never* forgive.

BETH

Do you want to tell me about it?

IDA

(Angry and anguished) What the hell's to *tell*? He died before I did, goddamn him! *(Crying)* He . . . *died*!

(BETH *attempts to comfort her, but is shrugged off.* MR. GASKINS *enters; seeing* IDA *in distress, he approaches her.)*

MR. GASKINS

Mrs. Purvis . . . is anything wrong?

IDA

(Snuffling) Everything is simply wonderful, you silly jackass!

BETH

Oh, Ida, don't be ugly. Mister Gaskins is trying to help!

IDA

I didn't ask him to butt in!

MR. GASKINS

But it's my job to help you if I can.

IDA

You can't! So butt out!

MR. GASKINS

Quite apart from my job, I'd like to help you as . . . a friend.

IDA

Oh, sure! Next you'll be playing "Hearts and Flowers" on the goddamned violin.

MR. GASKINS

I might if I could *play* the violin. *(No response)* But I *can* play you a game of gin. If you're a mind to. *(No response)* Perhaps Beth would locate us a deck of cards?

(BETH *looks at* IDA, *uncertain;* IDA *obviously wants to play cards but cannot bring herself to say so.)*

IDA

(After a long beat) You'd probably try to cheat me.

MR. GASKINS

(Playfully) I guess that's a risk you'll have to run.

IDA

Beth, get the cards. I'm gonna beat his silly young ass off!
(To GASKINS*)* It's for a penny a damn point, and I won't
take your marker! Cash money only, by God!

MR. GASKINS

Done!

(He sticks out his hand as if to shake, but IDA *knocks
it aside and in the same motion produces a five-
dollar bill, which she waves in his face, as* BETH
scurries off to get the cards.)

IDA

Now let's see the color of *your* money, Junior!

(Blackout)

Scene 4

(As lights come up the stage has the look of night. FLORA, *her purse in her lap, is in the chair facing the picture window and is reading aloud to* COWBOY *from Charles Dickens'* A Christmas Carol*)*

FLORA

(Reading) "A few of us are endeavoring to raise a fund to buy the Poor some meat and drink and means of warmth," the gentleman said. "We choose this time, of all others, when Want is keenly felt and Abundance rejoices. What shall I put you down for?" "Nothing," Scrooge replied. "You wish to be anonymous?" the gentleman asked. "I wish to be left alone," said Scrooge. "I don't make myself merry at Christmas and I can't afford to make idle people merry. I help to support the establishments I have mentioned. They cost enough, and those who are badly off must go there."

COWBOY

Dang it, that's enough!

FLORA

(Startled) Why, Mister Bennett! What ever is the matter?

COWBOY

I've heard all I need to hear about that sorry feller Scrooge! He puts me in the mind of too many other people. People that just wanta pack you off and . . . be shed of you.

FLORA

If you'll permit me to finish the story, Mister Bennett, you'll find that Scrooge undergoes a certain . . . benign conversion.

COWBOY

You mean he changes?

(She nods, smiling.)

Then I know dang well I don't wanta hear no more.

FLORA

But . . . why?

COWBOY

'Cause it ain't real! People don't change their hearts.

FLORA

Mister Bennett, I fear you miss the spirit of Mister Dickens' parable.

COWBOY

Who?

FLORA

Charles Dickens. The author of the story.

COWBOY

Huh! You can tell he never lived in Texas.

(FLORA *smiles and closes the book.*)

I dunno, Flora. Seems like people don't care about the other feller like they used to. There was a time when if a man's house burnt down, or his family got sick, or he had a runna bad luck of any kind — why, heckfire, his neighbors and kin come together and done what they could to help. People took *care* of each other. *(A beat)* Nobody shuffled you off to the side like you was some old railroad car they didn't have no more use for and just left you . . . to rust in the switchyards.

FLORA

Perhaps. But it may be that the past . . . always looks better from a distance.

COWBOY

Naw, dang it, people was *different* back then.

FLORA

I suppose it could be argued that people had to take care of their own in an older time. Not many places . . . like this . . . existed.

COWBOY

(Giving her a look) You think we're any better off for it? *(No response)* Are *you* any better off?

(*She hesitates, then shakes her head in the negative and looks down at her hands.*)

Then it don't sound to me like it's a very good argument.

FLORA

(Quietly) I miss my house. *(A beat)* I miss my house more than . . . anything. More than church. More than my car. Even more than my friends. *(A beat)* Not that it was all that grand as houses go. I suppose mine might be considered . . . little more than a bungalow . . . compared to many homes in Abilene.

COWBOY

Abilene? Say now, I usta ride in that big rodeo over in Abilene!

FLORA

I think I enjoyed it most in the spring and summer. I could garden then. Except during the worst of the sandstorm season, when it was all I could do to keep the grit off my carpets.

COWBOY

One year at that Abilene Rodeo I won day money in five different e-vents! Musta been around . . . 19-and-31. I recollect times was might hard, and that day money sure come in handy.

FLORA

I loved growing flowers. Lilacs and zinnias. Periwinkles. Morning glories.

COWBOY

Them five e-vents was bareback broncs, saddle broncs, bulldoggin', calf-ropin'. . . .

FLORA

And roses, naturally. Roses have been my favorite flower dating back to childhood.

COWBOY
What in tarnation was that *fifth* e-vent?

FLORA
I always yearned for outstanding yellow roses. I suppose because of that old song, "The Yellow Rose of Texas." *(She sighs.)* But, somehow, my yellow roses always lacked distinction.

COWBOY
I don't think it was bull ridin'. Oh, I rode a few bulls, but I never much cottoned to it. Seemed to me like bull ridin' was kind of a *fake* e-vent.

FLORA
Some said I should enter my reds in flower shows. But I grew them for my own satisfaction, not for accolades.

COWBOY
A workin' *ranch* cowboy ain't got no more reason to ride a dang *bull* than the man in the moon.

FLORA
I've never really understood why my reds prospered so, compared to my yellows. I gave them equal care.

COWBOY
So I'm satisfied in my mind that fifth e-vent wadn't bull ridin'.

FLORA
I admit I was shocked when my sons suggested I give up my house and come to . . . this place. *(A beat)* I had always assumed I would live out my life in my own house and die there. Perhaps just . . . not wake up one morning. I

hate to say it, but I believe they made interpretations of convenience. They had made up their minds I belonged here, and that's all there was to it.

COWBOY

Course, when I study on it, I reckon wild cow milkin' is kind of a fake e-vent, too.

FLORA

When I first realized my sons were becoming . . . increasingly inattentive . . . I foolishly blamed it on their wives. But it wasn't their wives.

COWBOY

I know *I* never had no call to milk a wild cow on a ranch. Or seen any other workin' cowboy do it.

FLORA

In truth, my sons had reached a point in their lives where other matters took precedence over me.

COWBOY

Still and all, takin' day money in five different e-vents ain't to be sneezed at.

FLORA

It's true I agreed to sell my house. But somehow I thought we were talking of . . . some time off in the future. The distant future. *(A beat)* But the next thing I knew, the boys said they had found a buyer, and the buyer wanted possession "immediately." So, before I knew what hit me, here came the moving van. *(A beat)* And the scavengers. *(A beat)* Picking over the . . . bones and relics of my life. Hauling away what they judged worth keeping . . . as if they had some *right* to do it.

COWBOY

Winnin' day money in five e-vents on *different* days is one thing. But doin' it like Cowboy Bennett done it is some-thin' that's . . . well, it oughtta be in Ripley's *Believe It or Not*!

FLORA

When we began talking about selling my house in late October, I had no idea — *none* — that I would be in this place by *Christmas*.

COWBOY

Christmas? Yeah, it's right on our heels. *(Looks at his watch)* It'll be official in about three more hours. *(A beat)* Merry Christmas to ya, Flora.

(She is startled back to the present.)

FLORA

And Merry Christmas to you . . . Cowboy.

COWBOY

(Enthused) Say, now, that's the first time you've called me "Cowboy," and I'm mighty glad you did! Why, ever time you've called me "Mister Bennett," I've looked around expectin' to see my daddy!

(They laugh)

By doggies, I think that calls for a celebration! We oughta have a drink on that! *(Then, remembering)* Except they took away my whiskey so dang long ago I can't hardly remember what it tastes like. *(A beat)* I sure would ad-mire havin' a little taste of that Wild Turkey bourbon.

FLORA

Would you settle for a cup of cocoa?

COWBOY

(Reviving) With you? Why, I dern sure will, and I'm much obliged.

> (FLORA *rises and after hesitating hangs her purse on the top knob of* COWBOY's *wheelchair; he notes it and beams.)*

Well, I'll be dogged! I'm comin' up in this world! I'm in charge of Fort Knox!

> (FLORA *laughs as they start toward the hall exit.)*

> *(Blackout)*

Scene 5

(As lights come up we see NURSE SYMMS, *who has had a hard night, talking on the telephone at the nurses' station; Muzak-sounding Christmas music is faintly heard.*

NURSE SYMMS

Calvin, you can make excuses until you turn blue, but that don't change me wastin' Christmas Eve night by myself in a honky-tonk fulla fanny-pinchin' drunks. My backside looks like a polka-dot dress this mornin'. *(A couple of beats)* No, and after last night you ain't *likely* to see it anytime soon. When you saw you couldn't get out of the house, you could of at least *called* me! That damn honky-tonk don't keep a unlisted number.

*(*NURSE BALDWIN *enters from the hall, pushing a cart on which is a large bowl of punch with a ladle and a stack of cheap, plastic see-through drinking glasses.)*

Tell ya what, Calvin: since you seem to like hanging around your house so much, why don't you just stay

69

there twenty-four hours a day for about a week? That way, if I take a notion to call your wife for a little heart-to-heart, you'll be real handy in case she wants to ask you any questions. *(She hangs up the phone.)*

NURSE BALDWIN
(Dryly) Peace on earth, good will to men.

NURSE SYMMS
That no-account four-flusher didn't even give me a Christmas present! And on top of that he stood me up last night. *(The telephone rings; she picks it up immediately.)* Calvin, you call me here again and I'm gonna make a certain call of my own! *(She hangs up the telephone.)*

NURSE BALDWIN
Would you really do that?

NURSE SYMMS
(A beat) I don't think so . . . but Calvin don't know that.

NURSE BALDWIN
Merry Christmas, Calvin, and may all your worries be great big ones.

NURSE SYMMS
I'll drink to that! *(She reaches under the counter, produces a bottle of vodka, and unscrews the cap.)*

NURSE BALDWIN
Selma! What are you *doing*?

NURSE SYMMS

Taking a little of the hair of the dog that bit me. *(She turns up the vodka bottle, takes a slug, and makes a terrible face.)*

NURSE BALDWIN

Selma, if Mister Gaskins finds out —

NURSE SYMMS

You gonna tell 'im?

NURSE BALDWIN

Well, no, but —

NURSE SYMMS

Hunny, that was strickly for "medicinal purposes." You wouldn't *believe* how sick I am.

NURSE BALDWIN

You'd better hide that bottle!

NURSE SYMMS

Splash me a little of that Methodist punch in one of those glasses.

NURSE BALDWIN

Sel-ma!

NURSE SYMMS

The bottle stays where it is 'til you do!

NURSE BALDWIN

Oh, God, I hate being scared! *(She rushes over to the cart, ladles a glass about half full of punch and takes it to* NURSE SYMMS *almost on the run.)*

71

NURSE SYMMS

(Pouring vodka) Want one?

NURSE BALDWIN

No! And if Mister Gaskins catches you —

NURSE SYMMS

He can't do a damn thing to me I'm not gonna do on my own.

(She drinks; through the remainder of the scene, she will periodically produce the vodka bottle from under the counter to sweeten her drink.)

NURSE BALDWIN

What does *that* mean?

NURSE SYMMS

It means, Hunny, that as soon as today's sad, crappy little Christmas party is over with . . . I'm a gone goose.

NURSE BALDWIN

You're quitting your job?

NURSE SYMMS

"Resigning my position."

NURSE BALDWIN

But how will you support yourself? And your kids?

NURSE SYMMS

Go on welfare. Steal. Print counterfeit money.

NURSE BALDWIN

Selma, be serious!

NURSE SYMMS

(Flaring) Don't push me! I haven't thought that far ahead! *(She takes a drink; calmer)* I just . . . woke up this mornin' knowin' I couldn't stand this Mickey Mouse place any longer. I've been here *six years*! And you know what it's got me? Like Tennessee Ernie sings: "Another day older and deeper in debt." And when I walked in here with my head throbbin' this mornin' and saw that Mickey Mouse Christmas tree with its sad little Mickey Mouse presents, I knew this had to be my last day for sure. *(She produces the bottle and sweetens her drink.)*

NURSE BALDWIN

Don't make a decision like that until you're feelin' better.

NURSE SYMMS

Hunny, I'm *workin'* on feelin' better. *(She drinks.)*

NURSE BALDWIN

Selma, you're gonna get drunk!

NURSE SYMMS

I certainly hope so! *(A beat)* When I started to work this mornin' I found two bottles of vodka wrapped in Christmas paper on my front porch. I decided right then and there God had sent 'em to help me through the day.

NURSE BALDWIN

Who *really* sent them?

NURSE SYMMS

A poor ol' liquor salesman who's wife don't understand him. *(She drinks.)* I think our crummy Mickey Mouse

Christmas bonuses is what pushed me over the line.
Twenty-five crappy dollars! If you stretch that out over
a year, it amounts to about seven cents a day! Seven lousy
cents *a day*!

NURSE BALDWIN

Oh, I wish you hadn't said that!

NURSE SYMMS

The truth hurts, don't it? *(A beat)* And my head hurts and
my heart hurts. I just hope the old poots around here took
their Lithium. I don't think I can deal with a buncha wild
old people actin' like house apes.

NURSE BALDWIN

If you don't quit drinking, you won't be able to deal with
anything!

NURSE SYMMS

I better start gettin' used to old folks. Won't be long 'til
I'm old my damnself.

NURSE BALDWIN

You wouldn't feel so down-in-the-mouth if you'd stop
drinking! Liquor is a depressant. It'll just make you feel
worse.

NURSE SYMMS

No way I can feel any worse. I woke up this mornin'
feelin' older than my grandmaw and too sad to cry.

NURSE BALDWIN

Selma, if I get caught in here —

NURSE SYMMS

I looked in the bathroom mirror, and I said, "Selma Bodie Blackman Burnett Symms, has it come down to *this*?"

NURSE BALDWIN

Selma, I can't take the risk. I'm getting out of here before we both get canned!
(She exits briskly; NURSE SYMMS *takes no notice.)*

NURSE SYMMS

I looked in that cracked ol' mirror and said, "Waitin' around some scabby hillbilly honky-tonk for a married man that down deep you don't give a *crap* about? Leavin' your poor precious children at home by theirselves on Christmas *Eve*?

(She begins to tear up.) Gettin' home too damn smashed to put your little boy's toys together, and just . . . dumpin' 'em boxes-and-price-tags-and-all under the goddamn Christmas tree?" *(She weeps.)* I said, "Selma . . . Bodie . . . Blackman . . . Burnett . . . *Symms,* how much longer are you gonna go on livin' a trashy life?" I said, "Do you wanta be known as Miss Trash-basket of 1981?"

(She produces a tissue from her pocket, wipes her eyes and honks her nose.) I didn't set out to be trash. I didn't come from trash . . . exactly. I'm *not* trash. *(A beat; archly and smiling through tears)* Did you know, in my soph-omore year, I come within seven votes of bein' elected Miss Leon High School Cantaloupe Queen? That's right! Just seven more . . . lousy votes . . . and Selma Bodie would of led the Cantaloupe Festival Parade right down the big-ass middle of Main Street. In a flashy convertible . . . and a long fancy gown. With the Leon Leopards Band marchin' along tootin' their butts off, and people wavin' and cheerin'.

(A beat) No tellin' where that mighta led. I mighta gone on to junior college . . . and maybe married a car dealer. *(A beat)* I nearly won out over a la-de-dah preacher's daughter! Little ol' *me*. With a shade-tree mechanic for a daddy. And a mama . . . that was a mama way too many times. *(A beat)* Just like me. *(A beat)* Everybody said for *sure* I'd win Miss Cantaloupe Queen my junior year. No sophomore had ever come as close to winnin' as me. *(A sigh)* But, we'll never know. I left school to marry ol' . . . what's-his-name. That first one.

(Shakes her head) Fell for a ducktail haircut and a pink Oldsmobile. *(A beat)* A *second-hand* pink Oldsmobile. With rhinestone-studded mudflaps. *(A beat)* And had my first baby so quick everybody started countin' on their fingers. *(A beat)* And me not much more'n a baby myself. *(A beat)* So . . . here I am! With three kids. All with different last names. And their daddies livin' in three different towns.

(She picks up her glass, drinks it dry, and extends it to where she thinks NURSE BALDWIN *is.)* Would you mind pourin' me — *(Realizing she is alone)* Never mind. I'll get it myself. *(She giggles, takes the vodka bottle from under the counter, pours her glass half full, then crosses to the cart to mix punch with the vodka. Crossing:)* Hello, you sad-assed little Christmas tree. With your sad-assed little packages . . . courtesy of The Golden Shadows Senior Citizens Home. *(Mixing drink)* Bow ties for the old men. Lipstick for the old ladies. *(A beat)* And none of 'em goin' anywhere but to bed . . . or maybe the graveyard.

(She takes a hit of her drink and stands looking at the Christmas tree.) Even if the old people around here get on my nerves — and they *do* — they deserve more than a sad-assed little dimestore fake tree like you. They got more comin' . . . than Mister Stingygut Gaskins and his

Ho-Ho-Ho bullshit and makin' 'em sing Christmas songs off-key. *(A beat)* Whole damn party'll be a fake. And sadder than . . . a baby's funeral.

> *(She stares at the tree for a couple of beats, suddenly places her drink down, and marches resolutely to the nurses' station counter; reaching under it, she produces her vodka bottle and yet another one still unopened. Then she hurries back to the punchbowl.)*

Merry Christmas, everybody! Golden Shadows is gonna have a *real* party for a change! (She begins pouring vodka into the punchbowl.)

> *(Blackout and end of Act One)*

Act Two

Act II, Scene 1

IDA (Joanne Burleson): Claude's the best damn smoocher I run across since my courtin' days.

BETH (Sara Van Horn): Well, you don't have to hog him!

CLAUDE (Edwin Stanfield): Don't fight, girls, there's plenty to go around.

Arkansas Repertory Theatre Production
Little Rock 1989

Act Two

Scene 1

(*From the dark we hear party babble: crosstalk, giggles, laughter. As lights come up we see the Christmas party in full sway; it is obvious the spiked punch is having its effect; all are drinking it. All patients are dressed in their best.* CLAUDE *sits on the couch between* BETH *and* IDA; IDA *is enthusiastically kissing him, while* BETH *covers her mouth and giggles like a schoolgirl.* COWBOY, *in his wheelchair at the downstage end of the couch, is twirling his lariat over his head;* FLORA, *in a folding chair next to* COWBOY, *drinks from one glass while holding Cowboy's glass in her other hand; her prized purse dangles from Cowboy's wheelchair.* NURSE SYMMS *is at the punchbowl, pouring yet another glass of cheer and shrieking with laughter.*)

COWBOY
(*Throwing his rope*) Yee-*hah*!

FLORA
Cowboy, I don't believe you took your Lithium!

(COWBOY *laughs and reels in the invisible dogie he has roped.*)

NURSE SYMMS

Hey, gang, ain't this a helluva lot better than singin "O Little Town of Bethlehem?"

COWBOY

Why, it's nearly as much fun as a dang rodeo!

IDA

Claude's the best damn smoocher I run across since my courtin' days!

BETH

Well, you don't have to hog him!

IDA

I'd marry him if he wadn't so damn crazy.

CLAUDE

Don't fight, girls, there's plenty to go around.

(*He plants a kiss on* BETH, *who goes into a fit of giggles;* IDA *then grabs* CLAUDE *and plants another kiss on him;* NURSE SYMMS *continues to shriek with laughter. Happy babble continues from the patients during the ensuing dialogue between the two nurses;* NURSE BALDWIN *charges in from the hall.*)

NURSE BALDWIN

Selma, we've got to get this mess under control!

NURSE SYMMS

Oh, don't be such a party pooper!

NURSE BALDWIN

Listen to me! Mister Gaskins just drove up to play Santa Claus, and I've had to put four patients to bed. What will we tell him is wrong with them?

NURSE SYMMS

Tell 'im they've got toothaches. *(She laughs uproariously.)*

NURSE BALDWIN

But they wouldn't all stay in bed! Miz Childress is trying to dance with her crutches, and Miz Reaves is beating her bedpan like a bongo drum and laughing her head off.

MR. GASKINS

(Voice over) Now hear this! All personnel and residents of Golden Shadows! An unidentified flying object has just landed on the roof of this institution and disgorged a fat man in a red costume! Our visitor looks jolly and friendly, so let's prepare to give him a warm Golden Shadows Christmas welcome!

(The patients greet this announcement with mock cheers, Bronx cheers and babble.)

IDA

If he gives me another tube of that greasy lipstick, I'll tell him where to shove it!

NURSE BALDWIN

All right, everybody! Listen up! Quiet! *(As the babble continues, she whistles shrilly.)* QUIET!

(They quiet down.)

Now I don't know for sure what's going on here, and I don't want to be told. But if you don't straighten up *right now*, Mister Gaskins could call off this party and send you to your rooms.

IDA

It's Christmas, for Christ's sake!

NURSE BALDWIN

Yes, and Mister Gaskins takes it *very* seriously. If you mess up, he might ask Doctor Gilbert to prescribe extra medications. Now we don't want that, do we?

(They mutter and shift, but the threat is effective.)

(To NURSE SYMMS*)* I've got to warn Mister Gaskins that some of the patients are . . . a little under the weather . . . and that Santa will draw a small crowd. Now *you* keep this bunch quiet! Some of us can't *afford* to lose our jobs.

*(*NURSE SYMMS *has suddenly had a turn for the worse; she stares blankly and puts a hand to her chest.)*

Selma . . . ?

NURSE SYMMS

I think . . . I'm gonna . . . be sick.

NURSE BALDWIN

Don't you dare!

(She gives NURSE SYMMS *a hard look and exits at a trot, turning downstage right.* NURSE SYMMS *wobbles to the overstuffed chair at downstage left and shakily sits; she reaches into the magazine rack, takes a newspaper and begins to fan herself.)*

CLAUDE

Cowboy, what you reckon's in that big package of yours?

COWBOY

I ain't got any idea, and I feel so good I don't much care.

BETH

You know what I think? I think it's a set of giant ceramic praying hands.

IDA

Now, who in *hell* would give anybody a set of giant ceramic praying hands?

BETH

A preacher might.

COWBOY

I don't hold with preachers.

CLAUDE

It's of a size to be a galvanized pan and water pump for a live-bait house.

IDA

God-a-mighty! That's even sillier than praying hands.

CLAUDE

Watch your tongue! Or I won't give you any more kisses.

BETH

(*Quickly*) I think it's whatever Claude says it is.

IDA

It's probably a lifetime supply of cowboy boots, or something just as stupid.

COWBOY

I'm willin' to settle for it bein' a big case of Wild Turkey bourbon. Or *two* cases of Coors beer.

CLAUDE

Colorado Koolaide!

NURSE SYMMS

(Sickly) Oh, God, not that!

FLORA

(Pleasantly) This certainly is excellent punch. I think I shall partake of a refill.

> *(She rises with great dignity, almost loses her balance, then walks with great care and deliberation to the punch bowl as* NURSE BALDWIN *rushes in from the hall.)*

NURSE BALDWIN

(Entering) Be alert, everybody! Santa Claus is on his way. Now you all just *behave* yourselves! *(Looking around)* Selma? *(Discovering her)* Oh my God! Don't you dare flake out on me now. *(Shaking her)* Come on, Selma! Pull yourself together!

NURSE SYMMS

I'll be fine. Just lemme take a little nap.

NURSE BALDWIN

You get on your *feet*!

NURSE SYMMS

Hunny, the Mayo Clinic couldn't get me on my feet.

NURSE BALDWIN

Oh, God!

MR. GASKINS

(Offstage) Ho-Ho-Ho! Ho-Ho-Ho!

_____

*(We hear the sound of a bell ringing as it approaches
from down the hall.)*

NURSE BALDWIN

Now let's be sure we give ol' Santa a great big welcome
and act like nice boys and girls!

IDA

Boys and girls, your ass! I could be your goddamn grand-
mother!

NURSE BALDWIN

Ssshhh, Miz Purvis!

*(MR. GASKINS enters in a ratty semi-Santa outfit:
scraggly white beard, red hat, red boots; otherwise,
he is dressed in a business suit. He rings a cowbell
wildly; NURSE SYMMS places her hands over her ears
and groans loudly.)*

MR. GASKINS

Ho-Ho-Ho! Merry Christmas! Ho-Ho-Ho!

IDA

(Mimicking) Ho-Ho-Ho yourself!

MR. GASKINS

Ho-Ho-Ho! Well, ol' Santa is mighty glad to be back at
Golden Shadows again, but he *is* disappointed to hear
that so many of our friends are not feeling well enough
to enjoy Christmas fellowship today. We'll just sing our
Christmas carols a little louder this year to make up for
the absence of our indisposed friends. Ho-Ho-Ho!

IDA

We're not singing this year.

MR. GASKINS

Not *singing?* What do you mean?

CLAUDE

We voted not to.

IDA

Ho-Ho-Ho!

MR. GASKINS

The Christmas committee didn't inform me of any such vote!

COWBOY

Course not. We just voted 'bout a half-hour ago.

MR. GASKINS

I can't believe what I'm hearing! We *always* sing at Christmas!

IDA

And it *always* sounds like shit!

MR. GASKINS

Mrs. Purvis, please! Will somebody explain what's going on here?

CLAUDE

We're tired of the same old sixes-and-sevens every Christmas.

COWBOY

We wanted something different this year.

BETH

And we're in a hurry to find out what's in Cowboy's big box.

CLAUDE

That's right! We've all been guessing what it is.

MR. GASKINS

We'll get to that in due course! But please, let's not scuttle our old traditions. *(Big false smile; cajoling)* Come on, I'll lead. How about that old favorite, "Jingle Bells" *(He starts singing.)*

> Dashing through the snow
> In a one-horse open sleigh
> O'er the fields we go, laughing —

(He trails off as they sit silently.)

(Vexed) Now *look*, people! Lifting our voices in song is a way we have of showing appreciation for so many bountiful blessings.

IDA

Such as my crippled leg!

CLAUDE

Such as the Mexicans being after me!

COWBOY

Such as livin' in a wheelchair!

(They laugh raucously; IDA offers her cup in a toasting gesture.)

MR. GASKINS

What has got *into* you folks?

IDA

Have a glass of punch, Santa!

(They all laugh.)

COWBOY

Yeah, if you wanta be one of the crowd, then have a glass of punch with us.

CLAUDE

(Slyly) Maybe then we'll sing with you.

OTHERS

"Yeah" .... "That's a fair trade" .... "Down the hatch, Santa!"

MR. GASKINS

Well . . . all right. Fair enough! *(He turns toward the punchbowl.)*

NURSE BALDWIN

Oh, Mister Gaskins, I wouldn't!

MR. GASKINS

You wouldn't? Why wouldn't you?

NURSE BALDWIN

(Hesitating) It's just . . . well . . . I don't care for punch myself.

FLORA

(Dignified) It's an *excellent* punch, and I say I shall have some more.

COWBOY

Atta girl, Flora!

(They all laugh.)

MR. GASKINS

(Pouring punch) At least I'm glad you're in high spirits about *something*!

(They laugh even more; MR. GASKINS tastes the punch.)

It *is* rather good! *(Takes another hit)* It has a certain distinctive . . . *tang. (To Nurse Baldwin)* Nurse, did you make this?

NURSE BALDWIN

Oh, no! No! I had absolutely nothing to do with it.

MR. GASKINS

(Lifting glass) Well, my compliments to the chef in any case.

(They laugh again as he drains the glass and pours another.)

COWBOY

(Singing)

> Jingle Bells, Jingle Bells,
> Jingle all the way . . . .

(All join him in singing raggedly; MR. GASKINS, beaming, starts patting his foot, keeping time with one hand and singing lustily at

Blackout.)

Act II, Scene 2

MR. GASKINS (Ronald J. Aulgur, as Santa Claus, after a bit too much spiked punch): It's *so* cruel when they mock my Ho-Ho-Hos! I went to Abilene to a Santa Claus school to perfect my Ho-Ho-Hos!

BETH (Sara Van Horn): There, there, there! Please don't cry! It isn't right for Santa to cry at Christmas.

Arkansas Repertory Theatre Production
Little Rock 1989

Scene 2

(As lights come up we see MISTER GASKINS, *as Santa Claus, pouring his heart out to* BETH *who, alone among the patients, is awake.* NURSE SYMMS *snores from the chair near the picture window;* COWBOY *and* FLORA *doze in place;* IDA *is asleep on the couch with her mouth open, and* CLAUDE *is asleep with his head on her shoulder.* NURSE BALDWIN *sits tensely on the stool behind the nurses' station.* MISTER GASKINS, *obviously tipsy, holds a glass of punch as he stands talking to* BETH, *who is on the downstage end of the couch.)*

MR. GASKINS

And that's when my daddy told me, "Son, don't be a damn fool. There ain't any Santa Claus." *(A beat)* Can you imagine telling that to a little innocent six-year-old boy?

BETH

It's a shame. Just a stinkin' shame.

MR. GASKINS

My sentiments zeactly. *Exactly.* Why rob an innocent
child of one of the joyous illusions of this life? *(Struggling
to control emotions)* All I wanted . . . was to be like other
children.

BETH

Of course you did!

MR. GASKINS

But my daddy wouldn't give me that fatissaction . . . *uh*,
satisfaction.

BETH

Bless your heart.

MR. GASKINS

It was bad enough to be called "Fatty" and "Lard Ass"
by other kids. But to be robbed of the lovely, nurturing
myth of Santa Claus by my own *daddy* . . . . *(He can't
go on.)*

BETH

Life is full of sorrow, Mister Gaskins.

MR. GASKINS

May I . . . tell you a secret?

BETH

Of course you can!

MR. GASKINS

It shames me to tell it, but it's the truth. *(A beat)* Daddy . . . drank strong spirits.

BETH

No!

MR. GASKINS

Oh, yes! Yes, he did. Daddy was a slave to Demon Rum. Which is why I have always e-chewed it. Pardon me. *Eschewed* it.

BETH

And wisely so!

MR. GASKINS

(He takes a big drink.) By the time I was ten years old I had made two vows. One, *never* to drink strong spirits. Which I have faithfully not did. Pardon me. Done. And, two . . . *(He can't remember and gapes blankly for a few beats)* 'Scuse me. Do you happen to remember what I was talking about?

BETH

Two vows. You made two vows.

MR. GASKINS

Yes. Thank you. And, two, to bring people happiness by playing Santa Claus every chance I got.

BETH

Oh, that is so *sweet*!

MR. GASKINS

Do you think I'm paid extra money to give up Christmas Day with my family and play Santa Claus here every year? *(A beat)* The answer is "No." Not one red cent. And what thanks do I get for trying to bring a little happiness into these . . . wasted old lives? *(A beat)* I get peed on. *(A beat)* People won't sing. *(A beat)* They mock my Ho-Ho-Hos. *(A beat)* They go to sleep. *(Bitter)* Look at this moth-eaten Santa Claus outfit. For fifteen years I

95

have got down on my knees and *begged* the board of
governors for a new and *complete* Santa Claus suit. And
every year they promise me I'll get it *next* year. And every
year I look more and more like some . . . ragged old . . .
half-assed Santa who couldn't even get hired by Wool-
worth's!

(He breaks into sobs; BETH *rises from the couch,
goes to him and wraps her arms around him; he
clings to her fiercely, crying on her shoulder.)*

BETH

(Rising) Oh, now, now, now, Mister Gaskins!

MR. GASKINS

Please call me "Santa."

BETH

Of course I will! Please don't cry, Santa. It isn't right for
Santa to cry at Christmas.

MR. GASKINS

Do you believe in me?

BETH

With all my heart!

MR. GASKINS

It's *so* cruel when they mock my Ho-Ho-Hos. I went to
Abilene to a Santa Claus school to perfect my Ho-Ho-
Hos. At my own expense! But do you think anybody
give's a rat's ass?

BETH

There, there, there.

MR. GASKINS

Sometimes I feel like just . . . *cancelling* Christmas at Golden Shadows.

BETH

Oh, you wouldn't want to do that. We'd be *lost* without our Christmas party! We really *do* look forward to it.

MR. GASKINS

Thank you. That makes me feel much better. *(He breaks the embrace.)* And I believe a tad more of that tangy punch might make me feel better still.

BETH

Let me get it for you, Santa. *(She takes the empty glass from his hand and goes to refill it.)*

NURSE BALDWIN

Uh, excuse me, Mister Gaskins. Should I try to get the patients back to their rooms, or what?

BETH

Oh, no! We haven't opened our presents. And we're all eager to see what Cowboy got.

MR. GASKINS

That's right. Santa's job is not yet done. Help me wake them up.

(They go around shaking people awake with varying degrees of success; COWBOY *and* IDA *awake alertly enough;* FLORA *wakes but continues to go on the nod;* CLAUDE *wakes but stares around blankly as if not certain where he is. Nobody even tries to wake* NURSE SYMMS, *who snores on.)*

Ho-Ho-Ho! Wake up and get your presents from ol' Santa! Ho-Ho-Ho!

IDA
I thought that Ho-Ho-Ho shit was over with.

NURSE BALDWIN
(Brightly) Did we all have nice naps? Do we all feel better?

CLAUDE
(Staring at Santa) Is that a Mexican behind that beard?

COWBOY
No, Claude, don't start that stuff!

CLAUDE
Lots of Mexicans at the Alamo had beards. Fierce-looking buggers, they was!

MR. GASKINS
Now for the pièce de resistance, Cowboy!

COWBOY
The which?

MR. GASKINS
The opening of your big present. Here, Nurse, give me a hand.

(He and NURSE BALDWIN *tug the package from under the Christmas-tree table to a position where the audience will have a good view of it.)*

COWBOY
Let's git on with it!

*(*NURSE BALDWIN *and* MR. GASKINS *rip into the package; all watch intently.)*

CLAUDE

Cowboy, if that turns out to be a Mexican cannon, you better watch for tricks. Mexicans is a terrible sneaky bunch.

BETH

If it *is* a set of giant ceramic praying hands, Cowboy, I think they'd look nice out front by the Baby Jesus water fountain.

COWBOY

It ain't no prayin' hands! It's somethin' real special! I feel it in my bones.

NURSE BALDWIN

Let's don't get our hopes too high, Cowboy. We wouldn't want to be real disappointed.

COWBOY

(Impatiently) Dern it, just git it open!

(All are silent and expectant during the final opening of the box. NURSE BALDWIN *peers in, as does* MR. GASKINS.*)*

NURSE BALDWIN

Well, would you just look at that!

MR. GASKINS

Here! Let's lift it out!

(They lift a saddle out of the box. It is almost as grand as advertised: well-polished, with silver plating, and altogether a handsome piece of work.)

BETH

Oh, Cowboy! How beautiful!

MR. GASKINS

Now do you believe in Santa Claus, Cowboy?

(COWBOY *wheels over to run his hands lovingly over the saddle; he appears awed; all are quiet during this bit.*)

COWBOY

(*Quietly*) Ain't that just about the purtiest thing you ever seen? It's . . . just like I recollected it. (*To* IDA; *triumphantly*) Didn't I tell ya, Ida? You was a dern know-it-all and wouldn't believe me, but ain't this saddle just like I said? See this here silver plate with words on it? Says, "All Around Champion Cowboy." Now whatta you think of that?

IDA

I can't read it from here.

BETH

Oh, don't be a sore loser, Ida!

IDA

It could say, "Stay Off the Grass" for all I can tell from here.

COWBOY

(*Laughing*) Naw, I got the best of you, and you know it! Here, let's put my saddle where even ol' Ida'll have to admit to it. Put it up there on the back of that sofa, just like you'd saddle a horse!

(NURSE BALDWIN *and* MR. GASKINS *grunt the saddle atop the couch.*)

Just look at that beauty! By ginnies, if Old Widder Maker was here, I'd show you *how* I won that saddle.

NURSE BALDWIN

(Looking in box) There's a card in here, Cowboy. *(She retrieves it and extends it to* COWBOY.*)*

COWBOY

Go ahead and read it.

*(*MR. GASKINS *makes another run on the punchbowl, weaving unsteadily as he pours yet another glass.)*

NURSE BALDWIN

(Reading) "Dear Papa: Hope you like this little holiday surprise. Uncle Buck's children helped me persuade him to give it up at long last. Take care of your health by eating right and getting lots of sleep. Love from all, Eloise."

COWBOY

Don't that just beat all! Why, I'd a heap druther got my saddle back than to get a three-speed electric wheelchair! They musta had to tie ol' Buck Ramsey down to git this saddle away from him. *(Wheeling about)* Somebody wake up FLora! Aw, never mind, I'll do it myself. *(Wheeling to her)* Flora, wake up! I got my saddle! Wake up and see my saddle!

FLORA

(Waking) Where's my purse?

COWBOY

Never mind your dang purse! I got my saddle back, Flora! I got my saddle! *(He takes off his hat and waves it wildly in the air.)* Yee-*ha*! Ride 'im, Cowboy! Ride 'im!

(Blackout)

Act II, Scene 3

COWBOY BENNETT (Macon McCalman): Why, if a hunnerd
people a day come to see my Old West museum, that'd be
twenny-five dollars right there!

FLORA (Jean Lind): Well, it *sounds* very grand. But sometimes
our plans don't always work out as we envision.

Arkansas Repertory Theatre Production
Little Rock 1989

Scene 3

*(The stage has the look of deep night; the nurses'
station is dark; lights in the hall are dim. It is long
past "Lights Out," and Golden Shadows is dark and
silent. We see* COWBOY *in his wheelchair, near the
saddle, which still straddles the back of the couch.
Though alone,* COWBOY *is talking.)*

COWBOY

Reckon I owe you a apology for losin' you in that poker
game. You might recollect that anytime I took on a
certain amount of whiskey, I become a bum judge of
cards. *(A beat)* Night I lost you to my contrary brother-
in-law I was so dang proud of a pair of deuces I raised
him three different times. *(A beat)* It goes without sayin'
my deuces didn't beat his jacks-over-nines.

(A beat) Thing that always stuck in my craw was I
didn't git to set you more'n a dozen times before I put too
much faith in them dang deuces. I wadn't about to get
you scarred up ridin' some old killer bronc. A saddle as
good-lookin' as you ain't got any bidness working rodeos. *(A beat)* Still and all . . . if Ol' Widder Maker was
here now, we'd give him a ride, wouldn't we?

(FLORA *appears at the hall door, in nightclothes and a robe, clutching her purse; she stops just inside, on hearing* COWBOY *talking.)*

Course I guess Ol' Widder Maker's been dead as a doornail . . . no tellin' how long. Horses don't even live long as people.

FLORA

(Uncertainly) Cowboy, are you all right?

COWBOY

(Startled) Good God, woman, you part Indian? You scared me half to death.

FLORA

(Crossing) What are you doing in here at almost *midnight?*

COWBOY

Nearly midnight for you, too, ain't it?

FLORA

I woke up so *thirsty*. I don't think that Christmas punch agreed with me.

COWBOY

(Chuckling) You couldn't get enough of that punch at the party!

FLORA

It gave me a terrible headache! I wonder if they somehow used tainted grapefruit in that punch?

COWBOY

(Dryly) Wouldn't surprise me a-tall.

FLORA

They should be more careful about such things. *(A beat)* I thought a cup of cocoa might help. Then I thought perhaps you might like some. But, much to my surprise, only Claude was asleep in your room.

COWBOY

I been in here thinkin'.

FLORA

It might appear to some you were . . . thinking out loud.

COWBOY

Oh, I mighta been. Sometimes I do that and don't even know it. Guess it comes from all them years I spent by myself in a line shack.

FLORA

If you prefer to be alone . . . .

COWBOY

Naw, naw. Glad to have you, Flora. Take a seat.

(She crosses to the chair nearest him.)

FLORA

(Crossing) The staff will throw conniptions if they find us here at this hour. I'm not sure why. I've always been perfectly able to sit in a parlor unattended heretofore.

COWBOY

Flora . . . I got me some big plans. I reckon you oughta know about 'em.

FLORA

Oh?

COWBOY

That first day you was here, you recollect me sayin' if I had my saddle back I might open The Golden Shadows Old West Museum?

FLORA

Well . . . yes.

COWBOY

Well, I *got* my saddle back. And I been thinkin'. If I was to charge everbody that come to see my museum two bits a head, that'd amount to a *goodly* bita money. Why, if a hunnerd people a day come, that'd be twenny-five dollars right there!

FLORA

Cowboy, that's a . . . lot of people.

COWBOY

Aw, I don't figger to git a hunnerd people a day right off! But if I had me some signs painted and posted 'em up yonder on Highway 80, and had me some *ad*-vertisin' circulars printed up, why, no tellin' how many folks my museum might draw.

FLORA

Well, it *sounds* very grand. But sometimes our plans don't always work out as we envision.

COWBOY

(*Enthusiasm mounting*) I might even ad-vertise on the radio! Why, if you turn on the radio in this parta the country you can't hardly hear anything but cowboy songs. And people that likes cowboy songs is purt-near a cinch to wanna visit a Old West museum!

FLORA

Wouldn't radio advertising . . . cost a great deal?

COWBOY

Well, I plan on *makin'* a great deal! Didn't you hear me talkin' about twenny-five dollars a day?

FLORA

Cowboy —

COWBOY

Ya see, if I was to keep my museum open six days a week, why there's a hunnerd and fifty dollars in my pocket! That's mighty good money. That's so dang much money that . . . why, heckfire, a man might even thinka gittin' out on his own again. A man might just . . . check outta this dang hospital . . . or prison camp . . . or whatever it is and git out on his own! I'm mighty tired of people tellin' me when to jump and when to squat.

FLORA

Cowboy, you're putting a big cart before the horse.

COWBOY

I don't have a doubt in my mind but what it'll work! Why, I know all there *is* to know about cowboyin'. I'll be able to tell them visitors to my museum so dang much about the Old West it'll put all them teevee and movie cowboys in the shade! Yessir! I'm gonna make me enough money to git out on my own again! Even enough money so's . . . somebody else might get out on their own again, too. *(A beat)* Providin' they was willin' to put up with a . . . stove-up old bronc rider.

> *(She stares at him for a couple of beats before grasping his meaning, then claps both of her hands to her face.)*

FLORA

Oh, Cowboy! That's not . . . that's just not . . . that simply isn't real!

COWBOY

We can make it real if you're a-mind!

FLORA

(Quietly) No, Cowboy, we can't.

COWBOY

Now, goddang it, there ain't a reason in the world —

FLORA

(Sharply) There are many reasons! We're *old*! We're finished! *(A beat)* That's the truth. I'm sorry. But you need to hear the truth.

> *(He abruptly wheels away, crossing downstage to the picture window and staring out. She rises, takes her purse and comes downstage.)*

(Crossing) Cowboy . . . I'm flattered by what you . . . suggest. Even . . . honored. And I do thank you for the sentiment. I truly do.

(He continues to stare out the window; she goes to the overstuffed chair and sits.)

You've been curious as to why I carry this purse around. *(A beat)* Fort Knox isn't in it, Cowboy, nor my life's savings. Not if we're . . . speaking of money. *(A beat)* The morning I left to come to . . . this place . . . I got up early. Before dawn, before my sons came to drive me here. Oh, they tried to persuade me not to spend that final night in my house. Everything was packed, you see. Most everything had been carted off to . . . here . . . and there . . . and the other place. But I insisted on sleeping there, because I wanted to say a private goodbye. So I moved a stack of boxes off an old couch and. . . .

(A beat) In the morning I told my house goodbye. Every room. "Goodbye, kitchen" . . . "Goodbye, dining room" . . . "Goodbye . . . *(She flutters a hand)* this room and that. *(A beat)* Memories tumbled in my head like . . . circus clowns on a trampoline. Then I went outside to my garden. I made some cuttings from my rose bushes. The yellows as well as the reds. I picked up a few small stones . . . a twig or two . . . and a rusty old key. Lord knows what it ever locked or unlocked. *(A beat)* And I put all that in my purse. *(A beat)* It's what I have left of thirty-six years in that house. That's why I always want this purse with me.

(Sighs) I thought I was . . . reconciled to coming here. I gave myself any number of little pep talks about it. *(Half laughs)* Oh, Norman Vincent Peale would have been proud of my "positive thinking." *(A beat)* But when I got here, the reality of it . . . the *finality* of it . . . was more than my mind could deal with. So I said I didn't belong here. That a mistake had been made. *(A beat)* No mistake was made, Cowboy. I knew that in my heart when I made those cuttings and picked up those . . . pitiful little relics.

(A beat) And I know it now. *(A beat)* And that is what is *real*, Cowboy. That is what is real.

COWBOY

(After a long long beat) Well, you don't hafta make no decision right this minute. Maybe after you see my museum you'll feel different.

FLORA

(Quietly, gently) No, Cowboy. No . . . no . . . no. . . .

(Blackout)

Scene 4

(Daytime; the beginning of a new work day. COW-
BOY's *saddle continues to straddle the sofa. We see*
NURSE BALDWIN *dry-mopping the day room floor;*
NURSE SYMMS *enters from the hall, appearing har-
ried and distraught.)*

NURSE BALDWIN
Well! Fancy meeting you here! I thought you'd become
a lady of leisure.

NURSE SYMMS
Shut up!

NURSE BALDWIN
And top-o'-the-mornin' to you, too.

NURSE SYMMS
Awright. I'm sorry. *(She goes behind the nurses' station
counter.)* Mister Gaskins just chewed up about four
pounds of my fanny and spit it out.

NURSE BALDWIN

You were expecting a medal?

NURSE SYMMS

Well, I didn't expect him to talk to me like I'm a yard-dog! He drunk as much of that spiked punch as anybody, the way I hear it.

NURSE BALDWIN

But he didn't *mix* it.

NURSE SYMMS

Look, I need a friend, not a smartass. That old craphead threatened to fire me!

NURSE BALDWIN

Yesterday you had your mouth set to tell him what he could do with your job.

NURSE SYMMS

Yesterday, hunny, I gazed on the wine when it was red. Today I woke up to the real, gray world. *(A beat)* Jesus, *I* didn't pour that punch down his gullet. He's the one that made a ass of hisself.

NURSE BALDWIN

Did you know he got so drunk he *cried*?

NURSE SYMMS

Knowin' that's the only thing that'll get me through this day.

NURSE BALDWIN

I didn't know what to *do* when he was saying all that embarrassing stuff.

NURSE SYMMS

God, is he on the warpath! Said he's gonna draw up a whole new set of rules and enforce 'em like a traffic cop and blah-blah-blah. Damn little dimestore Hitler!

NURSE BALDWIN

Not to take up for Mister Gaskins, Selma, but you don't know what all went on here last night.

NURSE SYMMS

Hunny, I don't even know how I got *home* last night.

NURSE BALDWIN

I had to load you in my car like a sack of wheat and drive you home! Mister Gaskins tried to help, but he fell down on the parking lot and tore his suit pants.

NURSE SYMMS

At least *some* good come of it.

NURSE BALDWIN

When I got back, he was crawling around the parking lot looking for his car keys. So I had to take *him* home and listen to more weeping and wailing about his mean old daddy. When I got back here a second time, Ida Purvis had peed a river in her bed —

(NURSE SYMMS *starts laughing*)

— and Miz Childress had bit her tongue trying to dance with her crutches —

(NURSE SYMMS *laughs louder*)

113

— and Cowboy was rolling up and down the halls yo-
deling about his saddle and trying to rope everybody —

(More laughter from NURSE SYMMS*)*

— and Claude had pushed all his furniture against his
door to barricade against the Mexicans —

*(*NURSE SYMMS *laughs on)*

— and we had to call Doctor Gilbert because Miz Clark
convinced herself she was dying of a massive heart attack,
which just proved to be massive *gas* —

(More laughter)

— and then two different batches of kinfolks showed up
to visit patients they couldn't have woke up by blowing
bugles in their ears!

NURSE SYMMS
(Wiping her eyes) Oh, God, thank you for that! I
wouldn't have thought I could laugh today unless I saw
somebody slap Nancy Reagan.

NURSE BALDWIN
Well, it wasn't all that funny if you had to deal with it.

*(*COWBOY *wheels speedily in; he now wears a set of
spurs on his boots, has a big red bandana around his
neck, and a rope coiled around one arm of his wheelchair.)*

114

COWBOY

(Entering) Either one of you gals wanta go to work in my
Old West Museum?

NURSE SYMMS

Cowboy, you've been talkin' about that damn museum
since the day I got here.

COWBOY

Aw, all that was just wish-talk. But now I got me back
my saddle, I aim to make good on it.

NURSE SYMMS

(Staring) Are you wearin' *spurs*?

COWBOY

Dang whistlin'! Ya like 'em?

NURSE SYMMS

What the hell good does spurs and a saddle do you if you
ain't got a horse?

COWBOY

Them spurs is part of my riggin' for my museum. And I'm
gonna git me a fancy-tooled western shirt with pearly
buttons and a new Triple-X Stetson hat!

NURSE BALDWIN

I don't know, Cowboy. . . .

COWBOY

Dunno what?

NURSE BALDWIN

It sounds to me like you might be turning into one of those drugstore cowboys you're always cussing.

COWBOY

(Uncomfortable) Well now . . . a man meetin' the public's gotta look his part. Folks comin' to see my Old West Museum would be mighty disappointed if they found me dressed up like a Dallas lawyer.

NURSE SYMMS

He'll be tryin' to get on teevee next thing you know.

COWBOY

Naw, dang it! Just . . . the radio.

NURSE SYMMS

Now where do you think you're gonna . . . *establish* this museum? In your room? With Claude hollerin' about Meskins and rattlesnakes?

COWBOY

Why, that little ol' room couldn't hold half the people that's comin' to see my museum. *(Looking about)* I been thinkin' . . . this here day room might be the place.

NURSE SYMMS

Well, you just think again, Buster! *I* run this day room.

COWBOY

(Grinning) I'm countin' on that! Figgered you might turn that nursin' stand into a saloon bar and pour spiked punch for my customers. *(He laughs.)*

NURSE SYMMS

Dammit, Cowboy, that ain't funny.

COWBOY

To tell the truth, I got my eye on that storeroom on the west side of this buildin' . . . I'm gonna speak to Mister Gaskins about it.

NURSE SYMMS

And just where do you think we'd store our extra beds and wheelchairs?

(MR. GASKINS *enters, carrying a clipboard; he looks most officious and severe.*)

MR. GASKINS

Why do we need two nurses standing around in here with only one patient?

NURSE BALDWIN

I was . . . just finishing mopping.

MR. GASKINS

Now that you're finished, I won't keep you.

NURSE BALDWIN

Yessir. *(She starts to leave.)*

MR. GASKINS

We're going to get cracking around here. I, as administrator, have perhaps been too much the Mister Nice Guy. Unfortunately, my good nature has been exploited. You will not be seeing much of Mister Nice Guy in the future.

NURSE BALDWIN

Yessir. *(She scurries to the hall and exits.)*

MR. GASKINS

Nurse Symms, exactly what occupies you at the moment?

NURSE SYMMS

I . . . sorta . . . just got in here.

MR. GASKINS

Hereafter, when not engaged in personally attending patients in *specific* activities, you will report to the administrator's office for additional work assignments.

NURSE SYMMS

Uh . . . yessir.

MR. GASKINS

Just now you may distribute fresh linen to the patients' rooms.

(She stands gaping at him.)

You *do* know where the linen room is located?

NURSE SYMMS

Yessir.

(She gives him a fearful look and scurries off; he makes a couple of checkmarks on his clipboard.)

COWBOY

It's about time things was run on a bidness-like basis around here!

MR. GASKINS

Cowboy, about your saddle —

COWBOY

It's a humdinger, ain't it?

MR. GASKINS

Very nice. The point is, we can't keep it straddling that couch. I'll have the nurses remove it to the storeroom.

COWBOY

I don't want my saddle in no dang *storeroom*! It'd git all scratched up and dusty! Maybe even mildewed!

MR. GASKINS

We can't keep it here.

COWBOY

Can't nobody *see it* in the dang storeroom! Besides, saddles has to be took care of. Rubbed with saddle soap and —

MR. GASKINS

Out of the question!

COWBOY

Set down a minute. We got to talk.

MR. GASKINS

(Checking his wristwatch) Cowboy, I'd love to chat with you but —

COWBOY

Goddang it, I don't want *chat*. We gotta have a *serious* talk. About my museum.

119

MR. GASKINS

Yes, what *is* this about a museum? Beth was in my office earlier saying something about a museum, but I couldn't make sense of it.

COWBOY

Oh, Beth's gonna run my cash register and sell my trinkets.

MR. GASKINS

(A beat) What?

COWBOY

Belt buckles. Bandanas. Ashtrays. String ties. Stuff like that. Beth's got a knack for meetin' the public.

MR. GASKINS

What *are* you talking about?

COWBOY

Set down and I'll tell ya.

(MR. GASKINS *hesitates, looks at his wristwatch again, and then impatiently crosses to the couch to sit;* COWBOY *wheels near him.)*

COWBOY

(Crossing) I've always had me this dream . . . to open up The Golden Shadows Old West Museum. Like that name?

MR. GASKINS

I still haven't the foggiest —

COWBOY

I figger to draw a hunnerd people a day after I git my signs posted and my circulars out and put it on the radio. Now when it gits started good, I'd be willin' to work out a bidness deal with ya. So that Golden Shadows gits fair rent, and maybe a little piece of my trinket bidness —

MR. GASKINS

Whoa, Cowboy! Hold your horses! *(A beat)* Are you proposing to open a *private* business at this *public* institution? Is that your pipe dream?

COWBOY

It ain't a dang pipe dream!

MR. GASKINS

Well, whatever you *call* it, it's simply out of the question! This is a church-affiliated, church-subsidized senior citizens home to provide restful care for the aged *indigent.*

COWBOY

Goddang it, I ain't no charity case! I pay rent!

MR. GASKINS

(Not unkindly) Cowboy . . . . your daughter pays a token amount toward your care. As do the relatives — if any — of our other patients.

COWBOY

And I ain't a dang "patient." I ain't sick and ain't never been sick to speak of!

MR. GASKINS

Well, "resident," if you prefer. The point is, Cowboy, if you own any property or have any income other than social security, you aren't even eligible to *be* here. You see, the church subsidizes the difference between what your daughter and your social security pay.

COWBOY

What's all that got to do with my museum?

MR. GASKINS

It has everything to do with it! You see, policy is made by a board of governors to conform with the rules set down in our original charter. And one of those rules — the *touchstone* rule — is that you can't be a property holder without disqualifying yourself for Golden Shadows residency. So even if I wanted to go along with your scheme, Cowboy, I couldn't permit it. And from the standpoint of simple practicality, we can't have people traipsing through this place and disturbing the lives of our . . . residents. This is their *home*.

COWBOY

It's my home too! So why can't I do like I dang well please?

Mr. GASKINS

(Quietly) I just told you why, Cowboy.

COWBOY

(Angry) I offered you rent! Even offered you a piece of my trinket bidness! Hail-fire, I offered you . . . a piece of my dream.

MR. GASKINS

I know you did.

COWBOY

(Angrier) If I make money, it stands to reason Golden Shadows makes money! Now, why would you say, "No," to a fair deal? You're always bellyachin' and poormouthin' about your dang costs and your dang budget! The old people around here ain't got . . . a pot to *piss* in! You could help 'em out!

MR. GASKINS

Cowboy, there are *rules*!

COWBOY

Yeah, and I know who wrote them rules! Salaried . . . gate-keepers like you! You wrote 'em to suit yourselves, not the people that lives here. We're just . . . *numbers* to you. So many to feed and so many to poke medicine down and so many to keep quiet and so many to collect so-much a head for.

MR. GASKINS

Now, Cowboy —

COWBOY

You think we was always a buncha old . . . *ghosts* that didn't amount to nothin'? Like you see us now? Mister, we had families and homes and bidnesses and jobs. We had dreams and plans, like everbody else. We fought wars and paid taxes, and we *cared* about things. *(A beat; much calmer)* And now we . . . we ain't got that. We ain't got anything to do . . . and the days pass slow . . . and we ain't got a . . . pot to piss in. *(A beat; trying to make a sale)* Aw, I ain't sayin' we'd get rich in thirty minutes! I might hafta put off that radio notion awhile, but I could post me some signs on Highway 80 and git my circulars out —

MR. GASKINS

Cowboy! Highway 80 is gone!

(COWBOY *stares at him, shocked, for a long beat.*)

COWBOY

What the devil you mean it's . . . "gone"? Why, thunder, I had my cripplin' wreck on that Highway 80, it ain't been but about four years ago. Some feller wouldn't dim his brights —

MR. GASKINS

No, Cowboy. Thirteen years ago.

(COWBOY *stares at him; a long beat*)

You've been with us almost thirteen years, Cowboy. Not four.

(COWBOY *abruptly wheels about and down to the picture window.*)

COWBOY

Naw. Naw, now, that . . . that can't be right. You're . . . jokin' with me.

MR. GASKINS

No jokes, Cowboy.

COWBOY

Five years, maybe. I . . . kinda git my dates mixed up once in awhile. Sometimes I can't rightly recollect just what year I won my saddle ridin' ol'. . . . (*A beat*) But it . . . just couldn't a-been. . . .

(MR. GASKINS *rises from the couch; he crosses to stand behind* COWBOY *and puts his hands on* COWBOY's *shoulders.*)

MR. GASKINS

Highway 80 became Interstate 20 about eight or nine years ago. It doesn't run through town any more. The new highway circles around us in a big, wide sweep . . . like Leon, Texas, might have some . . . contagious disease. *(A beat)* That was the purpose of the interstate system. To avoid . . . "unnecessary bottlenecks." That's what we are, Cowboy. You. Me. Golden Shadows. The entire city of Leon. *(A beat)* We're "unnecessary bottlenecks." So the world has passed us by . . . at about fifteen miles an hour over the legal speed limit. *(A beat)* Golden Shadows is nearly ten miles from the nearest highway now, Cowboy. And old Highway 80 that you remember . . . that proud old ribbon that used to run from California to the East Coast . . . is just a crumbling slab growing crabgrass. The kids use it for drag-racing.

COWBOY

(A long beat) How . . . old am I?

MR. GASKINS

You're coming up on . . . eighty-eight. *(A long beat; then, with false cheer)* Tell you what, Cowboy, let me get one of the nurses to bring you a little something to make you feel better. And later on today, after I've got my work laid by, I'll beat you at a game of dominoes. All right? *(No response)* That *is* a beautiful saddle. Maybe we can leave it here in the day room for a few days, until I can work out . . . something permanent.

(MR. GASKINS *turns away and exits.*)

COWBOY

(After several beats) Trouble with them teevee cowboys, ya see, Flora, is they don't tell the truth. My museum, now, it'll be right up to snuff when it comes to the truth. *(A beat)* I'll tell people all that gun-slingin' stuff's just not the way it was. Cowboys didn't wear guns in my time . . . and not near like they claim in the olden times. A gun can't help a cowboy do no work. And work is what ranch cowboyin' is all about. *(A beat)* Ain't that much to it, in a way. Cowboys spend half their time fixin' things it seems like they just got through fixin'. Work's always repeating itself. I don't believe there's harder work in the world, day in and day out . . . but it ain't a bit like they show on teevee.

(A beat) Bein' a ranch cowboy wadn't as much pure-dee fun as bein' a rodeo cowboy. I admit that. But in lots of ways I reckon it was better. Rodeoin's mainly for show. Ranch cowboyin' is . . . for real. The truth. *(A beat)* "The Golden Shadows Old West Museum." I like that name. Sure do. It's a humdinger of a name, ain't it, Erleane? *(A beat)* But it ain't the truth. *(A beat)* Shadows ain't golden. *(A beat)* Shadows just ain't . . . golden.

(NURSE BALDWIN *enters carrying a glass of water and a paper cup containing several pills.)*

NURSE BALDWIN

Cowboy, Mister Gaskins wants you to take these pills.

(COWBOY *keeps staring out the window.)*

Come on, now. They'll make you feel rested and relaxed.

COWBOY

You ever see a rodeo?

NURSE BALDWIN

Well . . . not exactly. I saw a donkey baseball game one time, and it was real funny. The players kept getting thrown off the donkeys and stuff.

COWBOY

Oh Christgodamightydamn!

NURSE BALDWIN

Now what brought *that* on?

COWBOY

Donkey baseball ain't the same damn thing a-tall!

NURSE BALDWIN

So I'm . . . culturally deprived. So shoot me.

COWBOY

(*Grumbling*) Christ Godamighty! Don't nobody know a dang thing about the Old West no more?

NURSE BALDWIN

Come on, Cowboy. I really don't have all day.

COWBOY

Young filly like you oughta see a dang rodeo before they quit havin' 'em. Maybe . . . maybe next time they rodeo over in Sweetwater, me and you can go over there, and I'll tell ya all about what's goin' on so ya won't come off a tenderfoot.

NURSE BALDWIN

Sure, Cowboy. Now take these pills for me like a good boy.

(She extends the two cups; COWBOY *looks at her extended arms but makes no move to take the medication.)*

Come on.

COWBOY
You sure got . . . mighty pretty arms.

NURSE BALDWIN
(Amused) Well, thank you, but if you think flattery will make me forget your medication —

*(*COWBOY *suddenly grabs one of her wrists, knocking the cup of water and the cup of pills to the floor. He begins to plant kisses up and down her arm; she screams and struggles to pull away, but he holds on doggedly and keeps kissing her arm.)*

Stop it, Cowboy! Are you *crazy?* Stop that! *(She manages to pull away.)* You tried to *bite* me!

COWBOY
No! I wadn't tryin' —

NURSE BALDWIN
(Indignant) Yes you did, you old idiot! You tried to *bite* me! I've never been anything but *nice* to you, and you started cussing me and tried to bite me! *(She crosses rapidly to the exit.)* I'm gonna tell Mister Gaskins you don't need pills, you need a shot! A *hypo!* We'll see how frisky you are then!

COWBOY

No, wait! I wadn't tryin' to bite ya! I was tryin' to —

(But she is gone; he trails off.)

— to kiss ya. *(A beat)* Your arms just looked so . . . so dang *young*.

(He sits for a moment, head bowed. Then he raises his head, looks at his saddle for a couple of beats and quickly wheels to the couch. Lights come slowly down. COWBOY *stares at the saddle. A spotlight on him and the saddle is now the only light. He places both hands firmly on the arms of his wheelchair and slowly and laboriously pulls himself upright. Then he grabs the couch. After a moment he slings one leg over the couch and, grabbing awkwardly, lunges into the saddle. He lurches, almost falls, but rights himself. Then, making an ineffective effort to spur his mount, he sits as tall in the saddle as possible and, grasping the saddle horn with one hand, he holds his other arm stiffly extended in the air like a rodeo rider as he takes his last ride.)*

COWBOY

YA! YA! YA! YA! YA!

*(Blackout
and
The End)*

The Golden Shadows Old West Museum

A Short Story by
Michael Blackman

THE LOBBY of Golden Shadows Rest & Care Home brought little excitement or comfort to Cowboy Bennett. The plastic chairs were painfully hard and the Holloway sisters demanded the old TV play only soap operas each afternoon. He was easy game for the nurses at pill time and somehow he was always running over the other residents' corns in his wheelchair.

But the lobby offered some refuge for Cowboy — at least it put distance between him and his roommate. Clyde Jenkins was eighty-five, rapidly declining in mind and body, and was convinced a moat ought to be constructed around the home to ward off rattlesnakes and Mexicans. He frequently awoke in the night and upset Cowboy by screaming that one or the other was about to get him.

Golden Shadows, a T-shaped, one-story structure of tan brick with a tar-and-gravel roof, sat on a dusty West Texas hill about a mile south of Sanders between the VFW and the rodeo grounds. It was home for about fifty-five aged. Two giant picture windows of the lobby faced west, for the afternoon sunshine. In the hot dry months of summer Cowboy often rolled his wheelchair to one of the windows and counted dust devils. Now, in the last days of autumn, long after the first frost, Cowboy would press closely to the window and search for cloud-banks building on the northwest horizon. When one was found, he immediately announced to all lobbymates:

"Well, looks like a norther's coming. Better get out your heavy garments."

Cowboy Bennett saw himself as a protector of Golden Shadows residents. He would not be living at the home except for the pickup accident three years ago. He drove a wheelchair now, had lost thirty pounds and he sometimes forgot exactly where he was, but he didn't consider these things major.

His daughter, Lisa, had urged him to move in from the ranch. She said with mother gone now he might fall down in a pasture and die before anyone would miss him. Ft. Worth was nearly 200 miles away and she just couldn't be checking on him all the time. But Cowboy preferred to chance ending up buzzard bait in some remote pasture. He finally gave in only after Mrs. Walters, the home supervisor, persisted that she needed someone like him to help look after the other residents — and after she promised he could move in his old cowboy gear. His room was decorated with a mounted pair of silver spurs, a rigging from his last rodeo, a bridle with rotting reins. All he lacked was a saddle.

"Know why they call me Cowboy?" He was sitting in his wheelchair in the lobby one afternoon, speaking to Grandma McAllister. She ignored him. The only others in the lobby were the Holloway sisters, holding hands and monopolizing the TV. "I say, do you want to know why they call me Cowboy?"

Grandma McAllister remained silent. In her lap she clutched a small black purse that, according to rest home rumor, contained her life savings. She in some ways was luckier than Cowboy. Most of her kids lived nearby, but she refused to live with any of them. After breaking her hip she lived alone for years, and had no trouble getting around in her wheelchair. Twice the town marshal had to pick her up for blocking traffic on the square when she wheeled out under the blinking yellow light. One day she journeyed almost a mile west of Sanders to the interstate entrance ramp. That's when the kids gave her the ultimatum: us or the rest home.

"Well, I'll tell you anyway," Cowboy said. "There weren't no horse I couldn't break. When I was at the Flying W, ranchers came all the way from West Texas to get me to help out. They'd give me a corral full of wild broncs and I'd have them eating sugar outta my hand by noon. I used to ride in that big rodeo at Stamford, the Cowboy Reunion. They still remember me over there, lots of the old ones do."

Grandma McAllister reached down and pulled up one of her sagging nylons, paying no attention to Cowboy. He reminded her too much of her former husband, who ran off in the early '50s with a beautician he met at a rodeo dance. The only other men in her life were her five sons-in-law, four of them wife-beaters. The other had gout.

The Holloway sisters were meanwhile totally absorbed with "Our Daily Bread," an unfolding drama of a college girl who didn't want to come home for Christmas and tell her mother, infested with cancer, and her father, an alcoholic infidel, that she was pregnant by her colored boyfriend. The sisters were near tears.

"They brought an old bronc from somewhere up in the Rockies that'd never been ridden," Cowboy went on. "Name was Widow Maker. Mean as the dickens. You'd be getting down on him in the chute and he'd try to bite your fool leg off. See he wanted to get you on the ground so he could stomp on your sideburns a little."

Cowboy laughed softly and rolled his chair closer to

Grandma. He leaned forward. "Well, we exploded outa that chute, me and that crazy bronc, and he did the durndest to throw me off." Cowboy was all excitement. "I rode him. And I mean I didn't ride him a few seconds like today's cowboys do. I rode him around that arena nine-and-a-half minutes by the clock. You shoulda seen that saddle I won. I'd have it here but I lost it in a poker game to my brother-in-law. It's got All-Around Champion carved on it. Anyway the crowd went crazy when they saw I wasn't gonna get pitched off. I rode ole Widow Maker till he collapsed, and then I got off and —"

"Oh, Mr. Bennett. Mr. Bennett." A nurse had entered the lobby.

"And then after I got off —"

"Mr. Bennett, time to go. Have to get your chores done."

Grandma McAllister took a blue handkerchief edged with white lace from her purse. She blew her nose and wiped her forehead. Cowboy was disoriented; the story wasn't finished.

"Get all those toilets on the north wing and you'll be through for the day," the nurse said.

One of the Cowboy's responsibilities, along with changing the calendars and filling up the Coke box, was visiting the north wing rooms twice a day to see the toilets were flushed. It was a health department safeguard against poor memory — not the most pride-building chore but Mrs. Walters said it was very important.

He rolled his chair into a hallway.

"Wilbur Bennett." It was Grandma McAllister, her voice as cold and cutting as a blue norther from the plains. Cowboy stopped his chair and spun it around. "I'm on to your tricks," she said, not looking at him.

Cowboy Bennett gazed at her and then turned around and rolled off.

"They're at it again," said the nurse back at the desk. "He's telling her that story about riding old Widow Maker. Today she's not even talking to him."

The others laughed. One of the younger nurses said, "Old people sure are something, aren't they?" Another nurse said wouldn't it be funny if Cowboy and Grandma McAllister got eyes for each other and started sparking on the sly. They might even get married. Somebody speculated on the sex life of geriatrics, to which the young nurse said get your mind out of the gutter.

"Oh, I wouldn't put nothing past these folks," asserted one of them. "Just last year we couldn't find Mr. Bennett one day. He'd disappeared from his room. Know where he was? In bed with old lady Martin. She's dead now. Anyway, all he had on was his boots and long underwear with the hatch open. She just had on her gown. I jerked back those sheets, and you should've seen them. They were giggling like two little kids playing doctor." The nurse paused and shook her head. "You can't put anything past these old people. They're more like kids than kids are. Watch them at the Christmas party. Believe you me, there's no place where Santa Claus is more alive than in the old folks' heads."

The next day a letter came for Cowboy. It was from his daughter, Lisa.

Dear Papa,
Just to let you know you'll be receiving a big box in the next few days. Don't you dare open until Christmas. Bruce has a bar association banquet and looks

like we won't get to come for the holidays. Be sure
to eat all your meals and do what the nurses say. I'll
call you Christmas Day.

All my love,
Lisa

P. S. The gift should make you the hit of the home!
Merry Xmas!

Christmas. Cowboy had almost forgotten. It was scarcely
a week away. And a big box was coming. This puzzled
him. He rolled his chair closer to the window for better
light and reread the letter.

A big box, he said again to himself. Hit of the home.
What the devil might it be? His stomach quivered. Always before Lisa had been predictable about gifts. Boots
three years ago, boots last year, white shirts two years
ago. And always she asked what he wanted. How would
she know what to get? She hadn't called in two months
and hadn't visited since last summer, when — he suspected — she had really come to see how her mother's
grave was being cared for. That visit was a bad one.

Cowboy was rooming with J. Grady Edwards, "Sr.,"
retired president of Sandero First National, who used to
glide through the halls in his electric wheelchair telling
everybody the mashed potatoes were better than laxa-
tives. Cowboy and the old man were always fighting. Mr.
Edwards had refused to let Lisa visit their room, so she
and Cowboy were relegated to the lobby the entire visit,
competing with television and the Holloway sisters. He
was glad when J. Grady Edwards, Sr., and his electric
wheelchair moved into the new nursing home in Abilene.
Cowboy suddenly stiffened in his chair and gripped the
arms tightly as he leaned back. His heart beat mightily,
as if he were easing down once again onto a wild horse.
It had hit him. Of course. Lisa was givinig him an electric

wheelchair for Christmas. With three speeds, no doubt. She had commented how nice they must be when she saw old man Edwards. Cowboy flushed at how nice and tricky his daughter was.

"Say, Clyde," he called to his roommate, who was peeking out the other window toward one end of the parking lot. "Guess what I'm getting for Christmas."

"Shh," Clyde said with a finger to his lips. He had an old army blanket wrapped around him from head to foot. "I think they're coming," he whispered. "My God, they are. They're taking my parking place!"

"Who's coming, Clyde?"

Clyde moaned softly. "They got my spot."

"Clyde, you know you aint got no parking spot. You aint been sneaking a little nip with Harley Wilson again, have you? Listen, I wanna tell you what I'm getting for Christmas."

"Those Meskins," Clyde mumbled. "Now they're coming inside. Oh Cowboy, what're we going to do?"

Cowboy looked into the parking lot. A battered '57 Chevy with reflector mud flaps and bumper stickers saying "God's Watching" and "Goat Ropers Need Love Too" had pulled into the lot. Catrina Valdez, a kitchen helper, was coming to work. "Don't worry yourself like that, Clyde. I once knew a bull rider who was a Meskin. Wiry little guy named Mendoza who could run faster and spit further than anybody I ever seen. He was real nice."

Clyde had his face pressed to the window to see where Catrina went. He looked over and said, "I read in the *Reporter-News* where they're causing trouble in the Abilene schools."

"Clyde, that was three years ago. They ain't even raised their hand to go to the bathroom since that bunch got thrown in the jug."

"They call themselves, CHEE-canos now," Clyde said, and shuddered. "They can really use them switch-blades."

"You're right," Cowboy said, scratching himself. "They're coming across the parking lot. I'll have to take care of it. You get back in bed, Clyde. I'll take care of everything."

"I don't know what I'd do without you," Clyde said.

"You better keep that blanket on," said Cowboy, peering out the window. "Those clouds are really building in the north. We'll have a real spine-chiller blow through here tonight."

Clyde got back into bed and Cowboy started for the door. "Just what are you getting for Christmas?" Clyde called.

Cowboy smiled. "A three-speed electric wheelchair."

The Christmas party was the event of the year. Committees and subcommittees were formed. Everyone was given some duty, however slight. The Holloway sisters were in charge of entertainment. Sadie McDonald, a former cook at Truck City, headed the refreshments group. Nellie Hawkins, the old local elementary art teacher, directed the decorations committee. Anyone bed-ridden or unspecialized would be put in Nellie's group, for the first step in making tree decorations required merely cutting construction paper in strips.

Cowboy was named director of transportation for the second time, which meant he had to make sure everyone got to the party. Fading memories required Cowboy to visit many rooms on the day of the party to remind residents. Even then many of them wouldn't show up until Cowboy personally came to lead them out of their rooms. Last year only old man Edwards missed. He locked himself in the toilet and wouldn't come out. This year Cowboy was after a perfect record. He prevailed upon Mr. Walters to see Grandma McAllister was named assistant director of transportation.

The Volunteer Fire Department of Sanders gave the home a Christmas tree. It was a perfectly shaped blue spruce from New Mexico nearly seven feet tall. The decorations committee encircled the tree with four strands of colored lights. Construction paper rings back-dropped with miniature Christmas scenes hung delicately from long-needled limbs, along with two dozen red balls surviving from last year. Atop the tree was a cherubic little angel boy with tin-foil wings and a golden halo. The little angel, which Nellie had made, held a hymnal and his mouth was open as if singing, his eyes painted reverently shut. A yellow light blinked from behind.

At the last moment, Clyde Jenkins and Harley Wilson pitched on a box of foil icicles without Nellie's permission. She was so mad she resigned as committee chairman.

"Hells-bells," said Harley, "icicles make it look real."

"No icicles ever looked like that — it's gaudy — all droopy and tangled," said Nellie.

Clyde said, "Long as I knew you and your mama, you two never could take a joke."

"Don't you dare bring my dead mama into this."

Peace came when some of the residents told Nellie her Christmas angel was the prettiest they had ever seen. They pleaded for her to take her job back. "I'll think about it," she said.

As the two men left the lobby Harley said, "Whoever saw an angel with no eyes?"

On the morning of the 23rd, a large box was delivered to the lobby of the Golden Shadows Rest & Care Home. It was Cowboy's, wrapped in brown paper and secured with twine. Immediately there arose among residents much curiosity and speculation. It was a stereo, a TV, a lifetime supply of cowboy boots, a half-dozen cases of Coors. Velma Roberts said it could only be a giant ceramic *Praying Hands*, but Harley Wilson said it was a galvanized pan and water pump for the live-bait house.

Of course Cowboy knew, but he wasn't telling. And Clyde knew. And he only told Alta Mae Givens. By sundown the entire north and west wings knew Cowboy was getting a three-speed electric wheelchair. "All the way from Cowtown," it was said.

That evening Cowboy dressed up in his best white shirt with pearl button-snaps and went down to the lobby. A half-dozen residents were inspecting the sea of gifts beneath the tree, including Grandma McAllister. Cowboy rolled up beside her. "Ought to be a good party" he said.

Grandma grunted.

Cowboy thought maybe her hearing was failing and said, much louder. "They say this one will be the best yet. Those Holloway sisters got a actor coming over from the junior college to put on a drama. And I hear the home's kicking in presents this year. Nothing fancy but something."

Grandma felt the Christmas spirit growing within her. Her daughters were coming after her tomorrow after the party and she would see Santa Claus come for the grandkids. There would be a big turkey for dinner, which, unlike that of the rest home, wouldn't taste like it came out of a can. She looked at Cowboy and decided to be half decent. "Mr. Bennett," she finally said. "Why'd you get me on that committee of yours?"

The question, even her speaking, surprised Cowboy. He cleared his throat and nervously picked his nose. "I thought you'd be right for the job," he said. "It ain't everybody that's responsible these days. I mean, if you came by my room and said let's go to the party and I didn't want to go, I'd probably go anyways. You got the grit to influence people. I'd be afraid *not* to go." He looked down and grimaced. "I mean, I think anybody'd want to go to a party you was going to."

Grandma was chuckling to herself. Both of them knew she was a threat to his position. She could fill the Coke box if she cared to, and flush all the toilets, and nobody had to tell her when the clouds were coming and when to get out her heavy garments. Sometimes she thought she would like to challenge him to an arm-wrestling contest. They could do it in the dining room so everybody could see. But then she took no pleasure in such things as looking for cloudbanks building on the horizon. The home, she concluded, needed somebody like Cowboy, however distasteful he was at times. "Anyway," she said. "I just want to thank you. I cut so many decorations last year that I got arthritis in my thumb and it still ain't well."

"You're mighty welcome," he said.

They talked a long while that evening, mapping plans for who would get whom to the party. Grandma would go after the menfolk and Cowboy the women, the obstinate and the forgetful. They talked about how they got to the home and about their families. Grandma observed that she must have at least thirty kin living in the area but, save two or three, they only came to visit on Easter, Thanksgiving or Christmas.

"That's the one bad thing about Christmas," she said. "You feel a little guilty about the things you should've done for people during the year. Everybody feels bad for old people at Christmas. I tell you, it must of hit the Seventh Day before the Good Lord could figure out his plan for the old ones."

Cowboy said yes, he knew what she meant. But he didn't really. He had only a vague notion of what she was saying. In fact, he forgot her words almost as soon as she said them. But the gist of what he felt compelled him to tell a story. It was about one of his foremen many years back who eventually got a ranch of his own. "His name was Homer, and he was sixty years old and never been married. People was always getting on him about his bachelorhood and he always just said he didn't want to rush anything. Well, one day he picks up and leaves and don't come back. Six months later he turns up with this twenty-year-old Meskin wife. Them same people who was getting on him about not being married really hollered, especially the church groups. They were going to see he got kicked outta church, but they finally found out he didn't belong to no church anyway. They said it was the worst thang they ever saw, marrying someone that much younger. And her a Meskin. Well, they had seven kids and he was still digging his own post holes till his heart gave out a couple of years ago." He winked at Grandma. "And they say we old folks can't cut it."

She thought he was getting awfully fresh but let it pass.

Save the two of them the lobby was bare. It was getting late. The colored lights from the tree flickered eerily off the green walls and a gusty north wind howled about the windows. The cold front hit and another — already paralyzing the upper Panhandle with ice and snow — was due tomorrow. Grandma and Cowboy sat in silence for a while. Then she reached over and tugged his sleeve. "Goodnight, Cowboy." she said. "I'm so glad you didn't talk rodeos. I never could stand the smell. Or them dances."

Cowboy remained in the lobby. He wanted to take a last look at the box that contained his mechanical wizard. It was the only electric wheelchair in the home, probably in town. He savored the possibilities. He could help set up races, against time, from the dining room to the lobby. He could organize a caravan of wheelchairs on Sunday afternoons, all tied together like a train, to parade before visitors.

Then it occurred to him. What if the box contained no wheelchair? What if it were *Praying Hands* or a live-bait house? He studied the box. It was laying flat, about three-feet by three and well over a foot high. Collapsed just right it would be perfect for a chair. He picked up one end. It felt light at first, no heavier than a case of beer or one of his old saddles. But he knew the newer chairs were streamlined and much lighter these days, and the batteries never came with them. So this would be about right. But he was still unconvinced. He finally loosened the twine, stretched it to one side, and tore back the tape holding down the brown paper and red gift paper underneath.

There was lettering on the end of the box: Contains (1) ea. 220542 Rocking Horse, Red Delux. *Godamighty.* Then he noticed the box was battered sōmewhat and had been opened before. What a scare! Lisa had gotten one of the kids a rocking horse and saved the box for future use. There was a hole near the flap at the end. Cowboy could see inside and he made the hole a little larger with his finger. He felt seventy years younger, and guilty. He couldn't feel much in the hole at first except the crinkled newspaper — then something smooth, soft and smooth, like fabric or simulated leather, the kind they often use on the backs and seats of wheelchairs. Quickly he rendered the paper and twine intact.

Just before turning in that night, he picked up his mounted spurs from the dresser and, trying to remember when he last used them, spun the little spiked stars, again and again.

The Golden Shadows Christmas party commenced promptly at five in the afternoon, almost the same time the first snow-carrying norther of the year hit town. The flakes were small and dry-looking and skittered around the porch. Darkness came prematurely and it was bitter cold outside. To the credit of Cowboy and Grandma, attendance was 100 percent. The perfumed ladies came in their dresses of flowered print. They had rouged cheeks and permanents newly set by a fleet of beauticians who had descended on the home that morning. The men, with what hair there was slicked down by green Fitch, came in baggy dark suits and skinny ties. The party might not have gotten off to such a rousing start except for the thoughtfulness of Harley Wilson, whose brother, Elmer, operated County Line Liquors. A fifth of Smirnoff's vodka found its way to the punch bowl and, though it wasn't much, it was enough.

More than just the Holloway sisters developed wet eyes when the junior college actor read a condensed version of *A Christmas Carol*. Cowboy was so moved he volunteered to meet Mr. Dickens in a dark alley. He felt nobody could have written about Scrooge's being so mean to a little crippled boy without being that mean himself. There was a near fight between Sadie McDonald and Old Lady Mashburn over who'd get the bows from the Christmas wrappings. Sadie vowed she'd pinch Old Lady Mashburn's head off but they were separated before she got the chance. Two old maids started kissing all the men, an unprecedented passion at Golden Shadows, and one of only two major setbacks for the men that evening. The other was Harley Wilson. Harley, who had stationed himself at the punch bowl for refill duty, suddenly took ill and toppled into the Christmas tree. They had to rush him to the bathroom. The residents said it was the Asian flu, but the nurses suspected the punch. The tree survived.

Then came the opening of gifts. Mrs. Walters called

names, and shaking hands plunged into work. The men ripped at the packages while the women cautiously picked at them so as not to disturb wrapping or bow. The home gave the women knitting kits and the men bow ties.

It was understood that Cowboy's box would be the last opened. As he lifted one end of the box with Grandma McAllister's help, the residents began to whisper. Realizing he was the center of attention, he suddenly looked up and said: "Y'all look here at Grandma. Don't she look purty? Smell that perfume? She smells ten times better than the best sheep dip I ever smelt." Everybody laughed, including Grandma, but she didn't laugh very much.

"I ain't got no idea what this thang could be," Cowboy said pulling off the last of the paper. "Well, look here. Says here on the box I'm getting a rocking horse!" After the laughter died, he opened the card taped on the end of the box. The front of the card showed a man on horseback in a snow-covered field, pulling a big evergreen from the woods with his rope. In the background was a little white frame building with belfry and holly in the windows, and there was a light glowing inside and smoke puffing from the chimney, and someone was standing in the doorway, waiting. The scene jarred Cowboy, but his memory focused no more clearly than a too-distant station on his old crystal set, barely here one moment, then faded away forever. There was a note inside:

Hope you like this little surprise, Papa. Mrs. Walters said it would be okay for you to have it. Uncle Ted was real nice about it. Merry, Merry Xmas. Sorry I can't be there. Don't forget, I'll call.

Love Lisa

Then Cowboy, in the happiest moment he could remember, opened the box.

They were stunned at first, all of them. Finally Clyde Jenkins said, "Boy howdy, a horse saddle. We got us a regular cowboy museum now."

And then everybody crowded around with oohs and ahs and ain't that nice and where're you going to put it?

"Gonna hang it from the ceiling and charge a nickel a peek?" Clyde asked.

Cowboy was shaking his head and grinning. His mouth was dry and he didn't know what to say. So it wasn't the three-speed wheelchair — but by George, they'd all have to believe him now, about him and old Widow Maker.

"Look," somebody said, "Got All-Around Champion — 1927 carved on it."

Cowboy looked at Grandma for approval. "That's real nice, Cowboy. Real nice." Then she spun her chair around. "I gotta go see how Harley Wilson's doing. Poor thang."

The snow turned out to be a heavy one, wet and sticky, and it was to make this Christmas whiter than any in recent years. Cowboy sat up late in his room after the party and watched the gentle whiteness settle on the windowsill and fields beyond. The home was quiet. Clyde and the old army blanket were securely entangled, and he was asleep. Cowboy felt awfully tired inside, and thought maybe the day had been too much. He was cold and began rubbing his arms, now bony and loose of flesh, no longer full of "sin and sinew" as his daughter used to say. He looked down to the shadowed heap on the floor, remains of the big box. Then he was startled.

"Why Mr. Bennett," a nurse said. "What are you doing still up? You shouldn't be staying up this late, not after a day like you had. Am I going to have to give you a pill?

Cowboy didn't answer.

The nurse looked around the room. "I hear you're going to make this an Old West museum and charge admission. I think a nickel's too cheap. You could run them through here a quarter a head on Sunday afternoons." She couldn't tell if he was listening but continued anyway. "I don't guess I ever saw a real championship saddle before. You know, one that belonged to a champion cowboy from the old days."

Cowboy hesitated. "Never saw one?"

"Nope, never did."

"Never even been to a real rodeo, I'll bet," Cowboy said.

"Not exactly, but I did see a donkey baseball game down at the ballpark. People were getting throwed off all the time."

Oh Christ Godamighty, Cowboy thought.

"Those donkeys just scared the daylights out of me," the nurse said. "If one of them kicked you in the head it'd hurt as bad as a bronco, wouldn't it, Mr. Bennett?"

"Probably would," Cowboy said. "Course you know that they didn't used to worry about having arenas filled with sand, so you'd have a soft place to land."

"My, my," the nurse said. "You really had to be a man to want to rodeo in the old days."

Cowboy, feeling sprightly, said, "That's what a lotta folks say." They both were looking at the saddle in the corner, completely refurbished, eternal token to the conquest of old Widow Maker. Cowboy noticed the nurse smelled nice. A new hairdo, he supposed. He liked her. He could tell she was really interested in the rodeo.

"Here, take this," the nurse said, holding a pill and a little paper cup before him.

Cowboy looked at the pill and the cup, barely discernible in the faint light, and at the smooth arm extended. Suddenly he grabbed her wrist, knocking pill and cup to the floor, and quickly pressed his toothless mouth to her arm.

The nurse was frightened, thinking Cowboy was mad about the pill and trying to bite her. "Mr. Bennett! Mr. Bennett! Stop it! Stop it I say!" But Cowboy held on, as determined as he would have been with a wilder creature in another time. And he was not biting. It was, as the nurse would tell the others at the desk, the wettest old gummy kiss you ever saw.

Larry L. King   Michael Blackman

Best known as coauthor of *The Best Little Whorehouse in Texas*, LARRY L. KING, as both essayist and playwright, consistently demonstrates an uncanny ability to use settings and characters from his native Texas to explore universal themes. Author of five plays, one novel, and eleven nonfiction books (including *Warning: Writer at Work* from TCU Press), King has won numerous awards for his writing and has taught at the university level.

MICHAEL BLACKMAN has been editor of the *Fort Worth Star-Telegram* for six years. Over the past twenty-five years he has worked as a reporter and editor for newspapers in Ohio, New York, and Pennsylvania. He is a native of Anson, Texas.